John Thomson

Descriptive Catalogue of the Writings of Sir Walter Scott

John Thomson

Descriptive Catalogue of the Writings of Sir Walter Scott

ISBN/EAN: 9783337388256

Printed in Europe, USA, Canada, Australia, Japan

Cover: Foto ©Andreas Hilbeck / pixelio.de

More available books at **www.hansebooks.com**

BULLETIN

OF

THE FREE LIBRARY

OF PHILADELPHIA

NUMBER 1

DESCRIPTIVE CATALOGUE OF THE WRITINGS OF SIR WALTER SCOTT

JOHN THOMSON

PHILADELPHIA

NOVEMBER, 1898

DESCRIPTIVE CATALOGUE

OF THE

WRITINGS OF SIR WALTER SCOTT

The Free Library of Philadelphia

PREFACE

♪♪

THERE is no question connected with the building up and administration of a free library that is more difficult of solution than how to make the greatest number of books accessible to the general reader. A student or a bibliophile, by reason of the variety of his reading and the gradually developed habit of consulting books of reference, rarely fails to find in a library not only the works or volumes which will most aid him in the study on which he may be engaged at the time, but his very habit of browsing amongst books will assist him in discovering in the library (however large) the volumes which will most facilitate his pursuit of knowledge and give to him the greatest delight. There are, however, regular students and persistent readers in a library to whom the mere abundance of material which a large library affords proves a hindrance, from the want of a sufficient number of literary sign-posts indicating the road of knowledge over which certain sections of books will carry them. This leads to the thought that there are many sorts of catalogues which should be accessible in public libraries. Without a great dictionary catalogue covering the whole possessions of a library, the institution would be practically a tractless desert. This, therefore, is indispensable in every

5

library ; but there are many by-roads of knowledge which require more detailed description than is possible to be found in the best prepared dictionary catalogue, however numerous the cross-references, or however careful the analytical work of the cataloguer. It is hoped that the preparation and issue from time to time of some descriptive catalogues of important series of works may prove of use, and by way of experiment it is proposed to publish as the BULLETIN OF THE FREE LIBRARY OF PHILADELPHIA, at irregular periods, a series of descriptive catalogues of collections of works such as have been published from time to time by important bibliographical societies, enterprising publishers, or book-loving collectors. There is no person who has been in the habit of using a public library who cannot speak with a certain amount of authority as to the value of the publications of the Roxburghe, Shakespeare, Cheetham, Scottish Text, Philobiblon, Surtees, and Early English Text, Societies. He will speak favourably of John Russell Smith's "Library of Old Authors," "The Chronicles and Memorials of Great "Britain and Ireland during the Middle Ages," published under the direction of the Master of the Rolls in England, the Vienna "Jahr-"buch," and many similar works; but who would say that the general reader in any free library had not much information to acquire which would be most useful to him if the contents of those works could be presented to him in an analytical form, readily accessible. It is proposed, therefore, to make an attempt to supply that want, and in order to render the FREE LIBRARY BULLETINS as generally useful as may be, they will be issued in parts, and an index added to each monograph. In this first number is given a descriptive catalogue of the writings of Sir Walter Scott, as published in that writer's "favourite "edition," in ninety-eight volumes. While this author's poems and novels are familiar to every English-speaking person, there is a residuum of nearly fifty volumes of other writings by Sir Walter which are practically unknown to a majority of readers. In the second number the series of works described will be the "Library of Old Authors."

The mass of works published and known as "The Rolls Series" now numbers over two hundred and fifty volumes, and is being peri-

odically continued. Without a general index and without the means
of concentrating attention upon the contents of each particular volume
by some such publication as the present, the works rescued from the
manuscript rooms of the British Museum, the Bodleian and other
great libraries of the world, become the working tools of only a very
limited number of readers, and a mass of invaluable literary material,
gathered together at great cost and with much labour, dealing with an
infinite variety of subjects concerning different countries and far distant periods of time, is practically lost. The writer had occasion some
years ago in pursuit of professional business to make a descriptive catalogue of about one hundred and fifty volumes of the Rolls Series.
The notes describing them and those describing Sir Walter Scott's
writings were originally drawn as a part of a proposed descriptive catalogue of the Irvington Library of the late Jay Gould, Esq. In undertaking the present BULLETIN it seemed a pity to lose the benefit of a
long but pleasant labour, the full end of which was not obtained, owing
to the death of Mr. Gould. Application was made to that gentleman's
eldest daughter, Miss Helen Gould, and with great courtesy she placed
at the disposal of the Trustees of the Free Library of Philadelphia the
manuscript catalogue as far as it had been completed by the writer
while he was engaged as private librarian to Mr. Gould. It is hoped
that various notes describing other large series of works which form
part of Mr. Gould's library, and copies of which have been acquired
for the Free Library of Philadelphia, will from time to time be
printed. The descriptive catalogue of "The Rolls Series" is nearly
ready, and will form Number Three of the BULLETIN.

DESCRIPTIVE CATALOGUE

OF THE

WRITINGS OF SIR WALTER SCOTT

Scott, (Sir) **Walter** (1771–1832), WORKS OF. Robert Cadell: Edinburgh. 98 vols. Post 8vo.

This is an Edition frequently called the "Author's Favourite Edition," and comprises the following sets of works:

		Vols.
WAVERLEY NOVELS	. . . . . .	48
POETICAL WORKS	. . . . . .	12
MISCELLANEOUS PROSE WORKS	. . . .	28
MEMOIRS OF SIR WALTER SCOTT; *or*, LIFE BY LOCKHART	.	10

It was originally published by Cadell, of Edinburgh, in 1830. These volumes are uniformly printed and bound.

This Edition of the Novels is embellished with "the Steel Plates belonging to "the original Edition [of Novels] in 48 volumes."

The Poetical Works have a fine series of illustrations by the celebrated J. M. W. Turner (1775–1851), to whom the subjects "were pointed out by Sir W. Scott when "that great artist visited him at Abbotsford in the autumn of 1830."

The Miscellaneous Prose Works include many which had not been previously collected or printed with the author's name, and the whole is "arranged (as nearly "as possible) in chronological order, thus illustrating the course of the author's "studies and exertions." They also are illustrated by Turner.

The Life of Sir Walter is written by his son-in-law, John Gibson Lockhart (1794–1854).

Sir Walter Scott's method as an author was to rise at five and commence work at six, so that by breakfast, between nine and ten, "he had done enough" (to use his own language) "to break the neck of the day's work." After breakfast he would work for two hours more, and by noon he was, as he used to say, "his own man." At one, unless going on a distant excursion,—on which occasions he started after breakfast,—he would go out riding, and an inflexible rule was to answer every letter he received that same day, unless the subject required research. In this way he kept pace with an enormous correspondence in a way simply marvellous when it is remembered that in twenty-five years he published twenty-five novels, several short tales, twelve volumes of " Tales of a Grandfather," besides the " History of Scotland from " the time of Macbeth to 1760," the " History of France," " Biographies of the " Novelists," the " Life of Napoleon" in nine volumes, and reviews and contributions to periodicals almost innumerable.

The Introductions to Scott's Novels are rarely read now, and could certainly not be written by a modern romancer; but more pleasant bibliographical gossip can hardly be fancied. As an illustration, the Introduction to " Quentin Durward" (Nov. xxxi., pp. xxv.–lxx.) may well be quoted, describing a visit paid to an imaginary French nobleman at the " Chateau de Hautlieu" and a dinner which would warm the heart of the veriest gourmet, followed by a pleasant account of a visit by Doctor Thomas Frognall Dibdin to inspect the library, and relates his lamentations over the books that were destroyed, his bibliomaniacal joy over what remained, with some amusing thrusts at the skill with which an account of them was included in his well-known " Catalogues of Books."

For convenience, the works and several articles included in this addition are given below in alphabetical order. The year after each work gives the date of its original publication. This, however, is "tentative" only, as even in Lockhart's " Life" one year will be given in the body of the work and another in the Chronological List of the author's works. The differences, however, are hardly material, and rarely amount to more than the substitution of one year for the next preceding or following. The several series of " Novels," " Poetical Works," " Miscellaneous Prose Works," and " Life" are indicated by the abbreviations " Nov.," " Po.," " Pr.," and " L.," respectively. The Roman numerals indicate volumes, the Arabic numbers refer to pages.

ABBOT, THE. 2 vols. (1820) . . . . Nov. xx. *and* xxi.

This is a Sequel to " The Monastery," and the events are laid in 1568, etc., in the reign of Elizabeth. The scenery and events described in " The Abbot," concerning Melrose Abbey, Holyrood Palace, and Lochleven will always make this novel an enjoyable book. The principal historical personages introduced are Mary Queen of Scots, the Earls of Morton and Murray, Margaret Erskine Lady of Lochleven, Catherine Seyton, Lords Herries, Lindesay, Ruthven, and others.

Sir W. Scott felt that " The Monastery" was not received with the favour accorded to his other works : therefore when he

" . . . had lost one shaft,
" He shot another of the self-same flight,
" The self-same way, with more advised watch
" To find the other forth."

The Notes contain a much larger amount of information as to the escape of Queen Mary, contrived by the son of the keeper, than is to be found in the ordinary histories.

" The Abbot" was a favourite with Sir Walter, and certainly the famous Lochleven and its Castle are glorious pictures as described by this master of pen-painting.

AIKIN, JOHN (1747-1822): VOCAL POETRY; OR, A SELECT COLLEC-
TION OF ENGLISH SONGS. (1810) . . Pr. xvii. 133

Two editions of this Collection were brought out almost simultaneously : one
by Mr. Evans, the bookseller, and the other by the original editor himself.
This is a review of both, published in the *Quarterly Review* for May, 1810.
See Evans.

AMADIS DE GAUL : POETICAL VERSION BY ROSE, WILLIAM STEWART.
(1803) . . . . Pr. xviii. 40
See Rose.

AMADIS DE GAUL : PROSE VERSION BY SOUTHEY, ROBERT. (1803)
Pr. xviii. 1
See Southey.

ANCIENT ENGLISH METRICAL ROMANCES, SELECTED BY RITSON, JOSEPH.
(1806) . . . . Pr. xvii. 16
See Ritson.

ANECDOTE OF SCHOOL DAYS . . Nov. i., xci.-xcvi.
See Scott, Thomas.

ANNALS OF THE CALEDONIANS, PICTS, AND SCOTS, ETC. (1829)
Pr. xx. 301
See Ritson.

ANNE OF GEIERSTEIN ; OR, THE MAIDEN OF THE MIST. 2 vols.
(1829) . . . . . . Nov. xliv. *and* xlv.

This romance relates to the Battle of Nancy, January 1, 1474, and the years
1474-7 in the reign of Edward IV. It afforded the novelist an "oppor-
"tunity of contrasting the wild nature and simple manners of the Swiss
"patriots with the feudal splendour of the Court of Burgundy."
Among the historical personages introduced are: Arnold Biederman, the
chief magistrate of the Canton of Unterwalden; Charles the Bold, Duke of
Burgundy; John de Vere, Earl of Oxford; Margaret of Anjou; René, the
troubadour King of Provence; and the secret tribunal of "The Holy Vehme."

ANTIQUARY, THE. 2 vols. (1816) . . . Nov. v. *and* vi.

This was Scott's third novel. It was "in correcting the proof-sheets of this
"novel that Scott first took to equipping his chapters with mottoes of his own
"fabrication," and in that device found an inexhaustible mine of home-
made quotations from "old play" and "old ballad." Six thousand copies
went off in the first six days. The story was published in a time of domestic
affliction, the period of Scott's eldest brother's sickness and death. The

oddities and humours of Jonathan Oldbuck, the Antiquary, gave many a reminiscent peep at the antiquarian propensities which characterized the novelist himself throughout life.

Scott says that this completed "a series of fictitious narratives intended to "illustrate the manners of Scotland at three different periods." "'Waver-"'ley,'" he continues, "embraced the age of our fathers, 'Guy Mannering' of "our own youth, and the 'Antiquary' refers to the last ten years of the "eighteenth century."

This novel was not so well received at first as its two predecessors, "Waver-"ley" and "Guy Mannering," but it soon rose "to equal and, with some "readers, superior popularity."

AUCHINDRANE; OR, THE AYRSHIRE TRAGEDY. (1830) Po. xii. 241–362.

This dramatic sketch was founded on the details "of the extraordinary case "of John Muir or Mure, of Auchindrane, who was executed A.D. 1611, to "which Sir W. Scott's attention was directed by Pitcairn, who was then about "to publish an account of the case in his 'Criminal Trials.'" The story which is told in prose in the "Preface" is a remarkable account of the crimes and turbulence consequent, at that date, on a pursuit of the "heathen-"ish and accursed practice of Deadly Feud."

[AUSTEN, JANE, NOVELS OF. (1821) . . . Pr. xviii. 209

This review, criticising "Northanger Abbey" and "Persuasion," appeared in No. XLVIII. of the *Quarterly* for January, 1821, and was inserted in Scott's prose works in error. It was written by Dr. Whately, afterwards Archbishop of Dublin. The article written by Scott was published in No. XXVII. of the *Quarterly* (vol. xiv. pp. 188–201).

Scott's article (which is not included in this edition of his writings) was a review on Miss Austen's "Emma," contrasting it with her previous novels—"Sense and Sensibility" and "Pride and Prejudice." Mr. Lockhart explains that the archbishop's review was readily accepted as proceeding from Sir Walter's pen, from the fact that the opinions of the two critics agreed thoroughly as to the worth of Miss Austen's books.]

AUTOBIOGRAPHY OF SCOTT, SIR WALTER. (1808) . . L. i. 1–84

This fragment, known as the Ashestiel fragment, was written by Sir Walter "in 1808, shortly after the publication of his 'Marmion.'" It gives a clear "outline of his early life down to the period of his call to the Bar, July, "1792." The Notes also are by Scott. He removed from Lasswade Cottage to Ashestiel, and thence to Abbotsford.

AYRSHIRE TRAGEDY. (1830) . . . . Po. xii. 241–362
See Auchindrane.

BAGE, ROBERT (1728–1801), MEMOIR OF. (1821–5) . Pr. iii. 441

This is one of the " Prefaces" in Ballantyne's " Novelist's Library." The author was a paper-maker by trade, and his letters on the troubles arising from taxes and strikes are entertaining. He employed his leisure in writing six novels. The first, " Mount Henneth," was sold to Lowndes for £30, and published in 1781. Miss Catherine Hutton, in some biographical notes on this writer, says, " It is, perhaps, without a parallel in the annals of literature, " that, of six different works, comprising a period of fifteen years, the last " should be, as it unquestionably is, the best."

BALLAD, IMITATIONS OF THE ANCIENT, BY MODERN AUTHORS. Po. iv. 89–388.

See Minstrelsy of the Scottish Border.

BALLAD, IMITATIONS OF THE ANCIENT : ESSAY ON. (1830) Po. iv. 3–87.

This is an essay written twenty-eight years later than the first issue of the " Minstrelsy of the Scottish Border," and "forms a continuation of the ' Re- "' marks on Popular Poetry'" printed in Po. i. 5–91.

BALLADS, HISTORICAL . . . Po. i., 293–428 ; *and* ii., 1–245

See Minstrelsy of the Scottish Border.

BALLADS, OLD, HISTORICAL, ETC. BY EVANS, THOMAS. Pr. xvii. 119

See Evans.

BALLADS, ROMANTIC . . . . Po. ii., 247–360 ; *and* iii.

See Minstrelsy of the Scottish Border.

BALLADS, TRANSLATED OR IMITATED FROM THE GERMAN, ETC. Po. vi. 289–359.

The following six ballads are here included :

Page

BATTLE OF SEMPACH. (1818) 332
First published in *Blackwood.*

FIRE KING, THE. (1801) 319
Written and undertaken for inclusion in Lewis's " Tales of Wonder."

FREDERICK AND ALICE. (1801) 327
First published in Lewis's " Tales of Wonder."

This poem (by way of memoir) was written by Sir W. Scott as president of
the Bannatyne Club, which was founded in 1822 for the publication or reprint of rare and curious works connected with the history and antiquities of
Scotland. Little is known of George Bannatyne. He compiled a MS.,
preserved in the Library of the Faculty of Advocates at Edinburgh, known
as the "Corpus Poeticum Scotorum," in which he has gathered together
"nearly" all the ancient "poetry of Scotland now known to exist." The
MS. is in a folio form containing upwards of 800 pages, "very neatly and
"closely written." This enormous labour was undertaken by Bannatyne
during the time of pestilence in 1568. The dread of infection had induced
him to retire into solitude, and "under such circumstances he had the energy
"to form and execute the plan of saving the literature of the whole nation,
"undisturbed by the general mourning for the dead and general fears of the
"living." Bannatyne is more fully dealt with by Scott in his article on Pitcairn's "Ancient Criminal Trials." (*See* Pitcairn.)

This, with "The Talisman," form Scott's "Tales of the Crusaders." This
novel illustrates the social confusion resulting from the long absence of the
Crusaders in Palestine. The romance is laid during the wars upon the Welsh
Marches, about the year 1187, during the reign of Henry II. of England, at
the time Archbishop Baldwin was preaching a crusade.

The novel introduces Sir Hugo de Lacy, Archbishop Baldwin, Henry II.,
Prince John, the Earl of Gloucester, and Richard Cœur de Lion. When the
book was all but printed and finished, author, publisher, and printer lost

heart and determined to cancel the work, and Scott began another story,
"The Talisman." But they were unwilling to sacrifice so much labour and
preparation, and the issue of the German fabrication "Walladmor," "which
"gave ground for suspicion that a set of the suspended sheets might have
"been purloined and sold to a pirate," put an end to all scruples, and Sir
Walter completed the two "Tales of the Crusaders," and the brilliancy of
"The Talisman" covered whatever deficiencies might otherwise have been
prominently recognized in "The Betrothed."

BIOGRAPHICAL MEMOIRS OF EMINENT NOVELISTS AND OTHER DISTINGUISHED PERSONS. (1821–1825) . . Pr. iii. *and* iv.

This is mainly a series of "Lives" written gratuitously as "Prefaces" to a
collection called "Ballantyne's Novelist's Library," published in ten volumes
in London, 1821. The series was to be printed and published for the sole
benefit of John Ballantyne. The "Lives" from that series with others
written for magazines here collected are—

A note on these several "Lives" will be found under the name of the
novelist or person whose biography is given by Scott.

The publication of the first volume of the "Novelist's Library" took place
in February, 1821, but the idea was apparently not prosperous, as with the
tenth volume the "Library" was dropped abruptly. Constable offered Sir

Walter £6000 to edit a new edition of the "Library" in twenty-five volumes, to be issued in a more attractive form, with twenty-five volumes of a "Select "Library of English Poetry," but the negotiation was never carried into effect. Scott did not believe that the old novelists could be made to pay in a serial form.

BLACK DWARF, THE. (1816) . . . . Nov. ix. 1–217

This was the first of the two novels forming the first series of " Tales of My "Landlord." Anonymity on anonymity was practised by Sir W. Scott. Not content with reserving as a secret the fact of his authorship of the " Waverley "Novels," he would not permit the "Tales of My Landlord" to appear even as " By the Author of Waverley," and they were published by a new publisher. With this tale begin the Jedediah Cleishbotham series, comprising "The Black Dwarf," "Old Mortality," " The Heart of Midlothian," " The "Bride of Lammermoor," "A Legend of Montrose," "Count Robert of "Paris," and " Castle Dangerous." Again a brilliant success was achieved, and Scott wrote that " Jedediah carried the world before him," and in six weeks nine thousand copies were sold; but " notwithstanding the silence of "the title-page and the change of the publishers, and the attempt which had "certainly been made to vary the style both of delineation and of language, "all doubts whether they were or were not from the same hand with "' Waverley' had worn themselves out before the lapse of a week." But Scott held up the mask, declaring even to his publisher Murray that he " did "not claim that paternal interest in them which his friends did him the credit "to assign him." The events of " The Black Dwarf" are laid in 1708, in the time of Queen Anne.

The prototype of the Dwarf was a David Ritchie, a native of Tweeddale, who was not quite three and a half feet high, of whom many particulars are given, Nov. ix. pp. xvii.–xxvi. The novel was reduced to one volume, having regard to the unpleasant characteristics of the Dwarf, though originally designed to occupy two.

BOADEN, JAMES: KEMBLE, JOHN PHILIP, MEMOIRS OF THE LIFE OF. (1826) . . . . Pr. xx. 152
See Kemble.

BORDER ANTIQUITIES, ESSAY ON. (1817) . . . Pr. vii. 1

This formed the Introduction to a richly embellished quarto in two volumes, entitled " Border Antiquities of England and Scotland, comprising "Specimens of Architecture, Sculpture, etc." It contains large additions to the information previously embodied in the " Minstrelsy."

BRAYBROOKE, RICHARD, LORD: PEPYS, SAMUEL, MEMOIRS OF. (1826)
Pr. xx. 94
See Pepys.

BRIDAL OF TRIERMAIN, THE ; or, THE VALE OF ST. JOHN : A LOVER'S
TALE. (1813) . . . . . . Po. xi. 1–141

This was published anonymously, and the critics, *e.g.*, the Reviewer of
the *Quarterly*, declared that the diction reminded them of a rhythm and
cadence heard before ; " but the sentiments, descriptions, and characters have
" qualities that are native and unborrowed." In the opinion of some, the unknown writer equalled if not surpassed the " Great Magician," and lo ! " after
" three or four years this and some other works published anonymously turned
" out to be the master's own compositions." This poem was written at the
same time as the poet was writing " the important poem ' Rokeby,' a new ex-
" periment" in writing two poems at one time, while also editing Swift's
works in nineteen volumes. It was intended to publish the two at one time,
but this idea was abandoned. At the suggestion of William Erskine, Lord
Kinedder, and in order to " mystify," Scott's Preface was " written over" by
Erskine with Greek quotations, etc., and the deception succeeded till Scott
removed the veil.

A sketch of this poem, avowedly written as " an imitation of a living poet,"
was published in the *Edinburgh Annual Register* for the year 1809. When
separately issued in 1813 it had been completed and largely rewritten.

BRIDE OF LAMMERMOOR, THE. 2 vols. (1819) Nov. xiii. *and* xiv.
235–392.

This was the first of the two novels forming the third series of " Tales of
" My Landlord." This series was written in the paroxysms of great sickness, by which most of the friends of the author feared that his life would
be sacrificed. The " Bride" was "not only written but published before
" Scott was able to rise from his bed," and he assured James Ballantyne,
the printer, that " when it was first put into his hands in a complete shape,
" he did not recollect one single incident, character, or conversation it con-
" tained." He remembered, indeed, the incidents of the story, but "not a
" single character woven by the romancer, not one of many scenes and points
" of humour, nor anything with which he was connected as the writer of the
" work."

Commenting on the death of heroines, Scott said, " Of all the murders that
" I have committed in that way—and few men have been guilty of more—there
" is none that went so much to my heart as the poor ' Bride of Lammermoor ;'
" but it could not be helped—it is all true."

The novel is founded on events which occurred in the year 1700, in the
time of William III., in the history of the Honourable Janet Dalrymple, the
daughter of James, first Viscount Stair, and sister of John, first Earl of Stair,
who was the chief author of the disgraceful massacre of Glencoe. Her
mother was Dame Margaret Ross.

Apart from dramatic versions, the capabilities of this story for the stage are
exquisitely realized in Donizetti's delightful opera, " Lucia di Lammermoor."

BUCCLEUCH AND QUEENSBERRY, CHARLES, DUKE OF (1772–1819),
    CHARACTER OF THE LATE. (1819) . . Pr. iv. 297

> This was published in the *Edinburgh Weekly Journal* in 1819. It is a
> warm-hearted eulogy of a good man who loved his country and won the hearts
> of all his tenants. In 1817 he abstained from going to London for the season
> and remained on his estates so as to employ nine hundred and forty-seven
> persons, exclusive of his regular establishment, on extensive improvements,
> and in that manner to afford relief to many poor families in that severe year.

BUNYAN, JOHN (1628–1688), LIFE OF. BY SOUTHEY, ROBERT.
    (1830) . . . . Pr. xviii. 74
    See Southey.

BÜRGER, GOTTFRIED AUGUSTUS (1747–1794). TRANSLATIONS OF
    "LENORE" *and* "THE WILD HUNTSMAN." (1796) Po. vi.
    291–318.
    See Lenore *and* Wild Huntsman.

BURNS, ROBERT (1759–1796), RELIQUES OF. COLLECTED BY CROMEK,
    R. H. (1809) . . . . . . Pr. xvii. 242

> This was published in the *Quarterly Review* for 1809.

BYRON, LORD (1788–1824): CHILDE HAROLD'S PILGRIMAGE; CANTO
    III. (1816) . . . . Pr. iv. 351

> This article appeared in the *Quarterly Review* of October, 1816 (vol. xvi.).
> It was written at a time when, as Lord Byron said in later years, "all the
> "world and his wife were trying to trample on him," and it required great
> courage to speak favourably of the popular scapegoat. Lord Byron fully
> recognized the service done to him in a letter he wrote to Scott in January,
> 1822.

BYRON, LORD: CHILDE HAROLD'S PILGRIMAGE; CANTO IV. (1818)
                               Pr. xvii. 337

> This splendid recognition of a splendid Canto, fuller "of deep thought
> "and sentiment though with less of passion" (*see* page 357) than Cantos
> I.–III., is amusingly characterized by Sir W. Scott in a letter to Lord Buc-
> cleuch (*see* Lockhart's "Life," vol. vi. p. 6) "as one of a series of miscel-
> "laneous trash" put together for various motives, which he details, the motive
> for this particular article being "the love of myself, I believe, or, what is the
> "same thing, the love of £100, which I wanted for some odd purpose."

BYRON, LORD, DEATH OF. (1824) . . . . Pr. iv. 343

> This was first published in the *Edinburgh Weekly Journal* of 1824. Scott on the day the intelligence of Byron's death reached Edinburgh went from the Court of Session to the printing office, and there dictated this article to James Ballantyne, and it was inserted without correction or revisal except by Ballantyne.

CALEDONIAN SKETCHES. BY CARR, SIR JOHN. (1809) Pr. xix. 160

> *See* Carr.

CALEDONIANS, PICTS, AND SCOTS, ANNALS OF. (1829) Pr. xx. 301

> *See* Ritson.

CAMPBELL, THOMAS (1777–1844): GERTRUDE OF WYOMING. (1809)
Pr. xvii. 267

> This review appeared in the *Quarterly Review* for May, 1809. It enforces the two views Sir Walter is known to have very strongly entertained: first, that Campbell was alarmed at his own reputation; and, second, that poetry should not be too carefully and frequently revised and amended.

CARR, SIR JOHN (1772–1832): CALEDONIAN SKETCHES. (1809) Pr. xix. 160.

> This review appeared in the first number of the *Quarterly* in February, 1809. It opens with an amusing account of an unsuccessful action for libel Sir John Carr had brought against the editor of a satiric work, entitled "My "Pocket-Book," written by Edward Dubois in ridicule of Carr's work entitled "The Stranger in Ireland." When Scott read the book complained of he first thought the action was not for libel, but for piracy in wholesale appropriations of other writers' paragraphs.
>
> The real cause of action was in the innuendoes of a caricature print used as a frontispiece. Scott hoped that he would not be sued for libel, as his severe review was not, "in the engravers' sense of the word, adorned with "cuts."

CASTLE DANGEROUS. (1831) Nov. xlvii., 243–466; *and* xlviii., 1–146.

> The period of the story is about 1306-7, in the time of Edward I. It is the second of the two stories forming the fourth series of the "Tales of My "Landlord." The incidents are derived from the ancient metrical chronicle of "The Bruce," by Archdeacon Barbour, and from the "History of the Houses "of Douglas and Angus," by David Hume, of Godscroft. They relate to the wars between Edward I., of England, and Bruce, of Scotland. The castle of the Black Douglas was so often "won back by its ancient lords, and with

"such circumstances of valour and cruelty, that it bears in the north of " England the name of the Dangerous Castle." The novel deals with the third capture of the castle from the English.

This was Sir W. Scott's last effort in fiction. He had told the outline of the story, in print, many years before in his " Essay on Chivalry." *See* Pr. vi. p. 36.

CHACE, THE. (1796) . . . . . Po. vi. 310
See Wild Huntsman.

CHATTERTON, THOMAS (1752–1770): WORKS OF. (1804) Pr. xvii. 215.

This essay appeared in the *Edinburgh Review* of April, 1804. The remarks on the extraordinary literary imposture of the Rowley poems are interesting reading, although many volumes have been written on the subject since Sir W. Scott's review of the first collected edition of this remarkable youth's poems, whose " life and death will be the lasting honour and the "indelible disgrace of the eighteenth century." Some of the principal impostures indulged in by Chatterton are usefully collected at pp. 232–234.

CHAUCER, GEOFFREY, LIFE OF (1328–1400). BY GODWIN, WILLIAM. (1804) . . . . Pr. xvii. 55
See Godwin.

CHILDE HAROLD'S PILGRIMAGE: CANTOS III. *and* IV. BY BYRON, LORD. (1816 *and* 1818) . Pr. iv., 351 ; *and* Pr. xvii., 337
See Byron.

CHIVALRY, ESSAY ON. (1818) . . . . . Pr. vi. 1

In 1812 Constable acquired the copyright of the " Encyclopædia Britannica," and in 1814 was preparing to publish a Supplement to that work for which Scott furnished two essays,—those on Chivalry and the Drama. The substance of these essays has since been incorporated with modifications into the text of the " Encyclopædia." This essay is included in the Chronological List of the author's writings under the date of 1814, but was first published in the Supplement in 1818. The writer received £100 for it.

The essayist treats of his subject under three heads: p. 10, the general nature and spirit of the institution of chivalry; p. 49, the special forms and laws of the order; and p. 106, the causes of the decay and extinction of chivalry.

CHRONICLE OF SCOTTISH POETRY FROM THE 13TH CENTURY TO THE UNION OF THE CROWNS, WITH A GLOSSARY. (1803.)
See Sibbald.

CHRONICLE OF THE CID: VERSION BY SOUTHEY, ROBERT. (1809)
Pr. xviii. 44

See Southey.

CHRONICLES OF THE CANONGATE. (1827–28) Nov. xli., 121, 238,
301 ; xlii., xliii., *and* xlviii., 147–430.

The first series included Mr. Chrystal Croftangry's biographical account
of himself, the reputed but imaginary author of these Chronicles, which com-
prised " The Highland Widow," " The Two Drovers," and " The Surgeon's
" Daughter." The second series consisted of " The Fair Maid of Perth."

The introduction to these Chronicles is exceedingly interesting as giving
Sir W. Scott's own account of the occasion on which he discarded the *in-
cognito* he had maintained as to his being the author of " Waverley." This
account was written soon after his financial ruin. He was a secret partner
with Messrs. Ballantyne & Co., the publishers, and on their failure stood in
debt to the enormous sum of from £120,000 to £140,000—say $650,000. To
pay his debts and retrieve his position he threw off the then almost open
secret, and at fifty-five years of age proposed to himself the task of discharging
every penny of his debts by writing and publishing even more vigorously
than before, were that possible.

He sold " Woodstock" for £8228, " The Life of Napoleon" for £18,000, and
before he died had reduced his debts to £54,000. These were discharged by
insurances, £22,000; cash in hand, £2000; and £30,000 advanced on the
security of his copyrights, and reimbursed to the lender within a few years of
the author's death. No similar story (except perhaps that of General Grant's
" Memoirs") can be narrated.

In Howitt's " Homes and Haunts" (vol. ii.) it is calculated that Scott's
writings produced to the author or to his trustees $2,222,000. If this is the
payment to them, what must have been the amount of money expended for
copies of his books by the public ?

CHRONOLOGICAL LIST OF THE PUBLICATIONS OF SIR WALTER SCOTT.
L. x. 269–276

CHRYSTAL CROFTANGRY: BIOGRAPHICAL SKETCH OF THE IMAGINARY
CHRONICLER OF THE THREE TALES ENTITLED " THE HIGH-
"LAND WIDOW," " THE TWO DROVERS," AND " THE SUR-
"GEON'S DAUGHTER." . Nov. xli., 1–120; *and* 238–242

For the tales, *see* each under its proper heading.

The sketch of Chrystal Croftangry's own history forms the introductory
story of the first series of the " Chronicles of the Canongate." Mr. Croftangry is the imaginary editor, and the lady, termed in the narrative Mrs.
Bethune Baliol, was " Mrs. Murray Keith, a dear friend of the author's."

See Kirkton.

This article appeared in the *Edinburgh* for July, 1805.

. Sir W. Scott deems that Ignotus and his Doctor friend may have done well to point out the dangers of various temptingly-described and richly-seasoned dishes; but to describe them and then stigmatize them as " unwhole-"some is only calling for the water-engine after you have set the house on " fire."

This article appeared in the *Edinburgh* for July, 1805. The writers were " the present and late housekeepers and cooks" to a Mrs. Hepburn. As the owner or proprietor of these two housekeepers and cooks, she was so amused by the review, that her husband, Sir George Hepburn, a Baron of the Exchequer in Scotland, gave a great dinner to Mr. Jeffrey and the literati of Edinburgh; but, unfortunately, Scott, who had thus " founded" the feast, could not be present to test the culinary powers of these ladies. The errata in the cookery-book quoted by Scott (*see* p. 106) include some amusing items,—*e.g.*, "*for* linen *read* lemon ;" "*for* chicken *read* onion ;" "*for* half a *read* three-thirds !"

This novel and its follower, " Castle Dangerous," form the fourth series of " Tales of My Landlord." Soon after the third series, consisting of the " Bride of Lammermoor" and " The Legend of Montrose," had been published, in 1819, some bookseller advertised a fourth series containing " Ponte-"fract Castle, etc.," and when John Ballantyne advertised in an Edinburgh paper that " Pontefract" was not written by the author of the tales in the first three series, the bookseller impeached Constable's authority, " asserting " that nothing but the personal appearance in the field of the gentleman for " whom Ballantyne pretended to act could shake his belief that he was in the " confidence of the true Simon Pure." The publishers wanted Scott to disclose himself, but he refused, saying, " Let them publish : that will serve our " purpose better than anything we ourselves can do ;" and so it proved, for " Pontefract Castle, etc., " fell stillborn from the press.

The story of " Count Robert of Paris" relates to the period when the Crusaders, under Godfrey of Bouillon, were before Constantinople, during the reign of Alexius Comnenus, Emperor of Greece, about 1090, in the time of William Rufus. It introduces Alexius Comnenus, Anna Comnena, his daughter and the celebrated writer of the "Alexiad," Godfrey of Bouillon, Hereward, the Empress Irene, Nicanor, Achilles Tatius, and Count Robert of Paris, the French crusader of the blood of Charlemagne.

The novel was almost entirely dictated to an amanuensis, as Scott was suffering from a stroke of paralysis.

CRIMINAL TRIALS IN SCOTLAND FROM 1484 TO 1684. BY PITCAIRN, ROBERT. (1831) . . . . . Pr. xxi. 199
See Pitcairn.

CRITICISM, MISCELLANEOUS. Pr. xix., 87–367; Pr. xx.; *and* Pr. xxi., 1–265.

CRITICISM ON NOVELS AND ROMANCES . Pr. xviii.; *and* Pr. xix., 1–86.

CRITICISM, PERIODICAL . Pr. xvii., xviii., xix., xx., *and* xxi.

CRITICISM, POETICAL . . . . . Pr. xvii.

CROKER, RIGHT HON. JOHN WILSON (1780–1857): BATTLES OF TALA-VERA, THE. (1809) . . . . . Pr. xvii. 291
This is a review of a poem by the well-known editor of "Boswell's "Johnson." It appeared in the *Quarterly Review* for November, 1809, and enforces Scott's dangerous theory that, to a large extent, the minor arts of composition and versification, such as "hasty expressions and deficient "rhymes, may be disregarded, as Falstaff did the thews and sinews and out-"ward composition of his recruits, provided the heart," which makes the poet as well as the soldier, is right. This is generally regarded as "flat "heresy" and an excuse for carelessness.

CROKER, RIGHT HON. JOHN WILSON: SUFFOLK, HENRIETTA, COUNTESS OF (1681–1767), CORRESPONDENCE OF. (1824) Pr. xix. 185.
This review appeared in the *Quarterly* for January, 1824. The corre-spondence covered the period 1712–1767. It included a wide list of cele-brated persons. The Countess of Suffolk, better known as Mrs. Howard, was the wife of Mr. Howard (the third son of the fifth Earl of Suffolk), was also the supposed mistress of George II., and afterwards became the wife of the Hon. George Berkeley, youngest son of the second Earl of Berkeley. The letters deal mainly with private affairs, and contradict many of Walpole's un-generous insinuations and allegations against Mrs. Howard.

23

CROMEK, ROBERT HARTLEY (1770–1812): RELIQUES OF BURNS, ROBERT. (1809) . . . . . Pr. xvii. 242
See Burns.

CULLODEN PAPERS, THE. (1816) . . . . Pr. xx. 1

This review appeared in the *Quarterly* for January, 1816. The rising of 1745, it must be remembered, had not become, in 1816, a matter of long by-gone history, and the inner story was still a novel matter. The account of clanship and its power furnished a subject on which Scott could write with good will and interestingly. The review contains many bright anecdotes of the Scotch, as (p. 11) where a pigmy Highland chief, warned by a clergyman that it was necessary to forgive an inveterate enemy, and who further supported his argument by the scriptural expression, "Vengeance is Mine, saith "the Lord," received for an answer, accompanied by a deep sigh, "To be "sure, it is too sweet a morsel for a mortal;" and, added the acquiescing penitent, "Well, I forgive him; but the deil take you, Donald" (turning to his son), "if you forgive him."

CUMBERLAND, RICHARD (1732–1811): JOHN DE LANCASTER: A NOVEL. (1809) . . . . . Pr. xxviii. 138

This appeared in the *Quarterly Review* for 1809. The novel was written when Cumberland was seventy-six years of age.

CUMBERLAND, RICHARD, MEMOIR OF. (1821–5) . . Pr. iii. 191

This is one of the "Prefaces" in Ballantyne's "Novelist's Library." This dramatic author and essayist was the grandson of "Bentley, the renowned "critic," who was styled by Goldsmith "The Terence of England, the "Mender of Hearts." He was a very voluminous writer, the following works amongst others being attributed to his pen: two epics, thirty-eight dramatic pieces, three controversial publications, three novels, nine miscellaneous and prose works, besides twenty-three fugitive pieces. His first novel, "Arundel," was written at Brighton in a few weeks, and sent to the press in parcels as he wrote it. Goldsmith, in his epitaph on Cumberland, describes him as,—

> "A flattering painter, who made it his care
> "To draw men as they ought to be, not as they are.
> "His gallants are all faultless, his women divine,
> "And Comedy wonders at being so fine;
>
>   *   *   *   *   *
>
> "Say, where has one poet this malady caught,
> "Or, wherefore his characters thus without fault?"

CURRENCY, THE: LETTERS FROM MALAGROWTHER, MALACHI. (1826) Pr. xxi. 267–402

See Malagrowther.

CURSE OF KEHAMA. BY SOUTHEY, ROBERT. (1811) Pr. xvii. 301

See Southey.

DAVY, SIR HUMPHRY (1778-1829): SALMONIA; OR, DAYS OF FLY-
FISHING. (1828) . . . . . Pr. xx. 245

See Salmonia.

DEATH OF THE LAIRD'S JOCK. (1828) . . Nov. xli. 375-385

This was the last of three sketches published in "The Keepsake" for
1828. The period of the story is laid in the year 1600, in the reign of Elizabeth. It is in the form of a letter to the editor of "The Keepsake" by "The
"Author of Waverley."

DE FOE, DANIEL (1661-1731), MEMOIR OF. (1821-5) Pr. iv. 228

This sketch was written by John Ballantyne, the Edinburgh bookseller, to
which Sir W. Scott added some critical notices comprising an excellent
account (pp. 266-274) of Defoe's scheme to effect a sale of Drelincourt's
book on "The Fear of Death," by the invention and addition of "Mrs.
"Veal's Apparition."

Two appendixes are added,—viz., "Some Account of Alexander Selkirk"-
(pp. 282-287), and the "Apparition of Mrs. Veal" (pp. 288-296).

De Foe's political works occasioned him "much suffering and pecuniary
"loss," which he summed up in this couplet:

> "No man has tasted differing fortunes more,
> "And thirteen times I have been rich and poor."

DEMONOLOGY AND WITCHCRAFT, LETTERS ON. (1830.)

These originally formed part of Murray's "Family Library," where copies
can be found. They are included in some editions (the one hundred volumes
edition, for instance) of Scott's writings to complete the collection of his prose
works, but are omitted in this ninety-eight volumes edition.

DIARY OF A VOYAGE IN THE LIGHTHOUSE YACHT TO NOVA ZEMBLA
AND THE LORD KNOWS WHERE. (1814) L. iv. 182-370

This is a diary "contained in five little paper books," written in the summer
of 1814, describing a six weeks' pleasure voyage, wherein, "according to the
"scene and occasion," we have before us "the poet, the antiquary, the magis-
"trate, the planter, and the agriculturist, but everywhere the warm yet saga-
"cious philanthropist." It is a delightful piece of autobiography.

25

DISCOURSES, TWO RELIGIOUS. (1828.)

    See Religious.

DONAT, MRS.: COOKERY, THE NEW PRACTICE OF. (1805) Pr. xix. 100

    See Cookery.

DOOM OF DEVORGOIL, THE. (1830) . . . Po. xii. 113–240

    This was written for Daniel Terry (1780–1829), of the Adelphi Theatre,
London, who was, during many years, on terms of intimacy with Sir W.
Scott. The general story of the " Doom of Devorgoil" is founded on an old
Scottish tradition, the scene of which lies in Galloway. It did not succeed
on the stage.

DRAMA, THE, ESSAY ON. (1819) . . . . Pr. v. 217

    This is included in Scott's " Chronological List of Writings" under the
year 1814. It was first published in the " Supplement to the Encyclopædia
" Britannica," in 1819. Sir Walter received £100 for the essay.

    The essayist treats of his subject under certain broad heads,—*e.g.*: (p. 221)
Grecian theatrical representations; (p. 258) the Roman drama; (p. 266) the
modern drama as developed in Italy; (p. 293) the drama in France; (p. 331)
the drama in England from the revival of the theatre until the great Civil
War; (p. 352) from the Restoration to the reign of Queen Anne; (p. 365)
from the earlier part of the eighteenth century to the time of George the
Fourth; (p. 376) the period of David Garrick, Sheridan, the elder Colman,
Mrs. Siddons, Kean, Young, and Miss O'Neil. (*See* Chivalry.)

DRYDEN, JOHN (1631–1700), THE LIFE OF. (1808) . . Pr. i.

    The " Life and Works of Dryden, with Notes," were published by Scott in
eighteen volumes, for which the editor's fee was forty guineas a volume,—*i.e.*,
£756. It was reviewed with great praise by Henry Hallam in the *Edinburgh
Review* for October, 1808.

    A view of Carlisle after J. M. W. Turner by E. Goodall is given as frontis-
piece, and a view of the poet's tomb in Westminster Abbey, also after J. M.
W. Turner by J. Horsburgh, is added.

DURHAM GARLAND . . L. v. 397–408

    See Guy Mannering.

ELLIS, GEORGE (1745–1815): SPECIMENS OF EARLY ENGLISH METRICAL
    ROMANCES. (1806) . . . . . Pr. xvii. 16

    This is an article published in the *Edinburgh Review* for 1806, contrasting
the " Metrical Romances" edited by Joseph Ritson with those edited by Mr.
Ellis.

ELLIS, GEORGE: SPECIMENS OF THE EARLY ENGLISH POETS. (1804)
Pr. xvii. 1

George Ellis became the friend of Sir W. Scott in the year 1800. The essay from which these remarks are taken appeared in the *Edinburgh Review* for 1804.

ENGLISH SONGS, VOCAL POETRY; OR, A SELECT COLLECTION OF. BY JOHN AIKIN. (1810) . . . . Pr. xvii. 133

See Aikin.

EVANS, THOMAS: OLD BALLADS, HISTORICAL, ETC. (1810) Pr. xvii. 119.

This was published in the *Quarterly Review*, May, 1810. It reviews an edition of poems revised by the poet's son, R. H. Evans. The article also criticises Aikin's "Vocal Poetry." (*See* Aikin.)

EYRBIGGIA-SAGA, ABSTRACT OF THE. (1814) . . Pr. v. 355

These are "the early annals of that district of Iceland lying around the "promontory called Snæfells." The essay was contributed by Sir W. Scott to Robert Jameson's "Illustrations of Northern Antiquities," published in the summer of 1814. Sir W. Scott was of opinion that the stone circles such as are seen at Stennis and Stonehenge were erections among the northern nations to mark their places of meeting, whether for religious purposes or civil policy. But as to how such stones were "raised, transported, and placed upright," he has no other solution than the usual answer, that "that is a puzzling question." (*See* L. iv. 265.)

FAIR MAID OF PERTH, THE; OR, SAINT VALENTINE'S DAY. 2 vols. (1828) . . . . . . Nov. xlii. *and* xliii.

This formed the second series of "The Chronicles of the Canongate." The story is laid in Perth and its vicinity in the year 1402 in the time of Henry IV. of England and of Robert III. of Scotland. The story includes the settlement of a feud between two clans by a combat between thirty of their chosen warriors, in King Robert's presence, on Palm Sunday. "The novel "had a favourable reception." The second title arises from the incident that Catharine, the daughter of the old glover of Perth, kisses Henry Smith, while asleep, on St. Valentine's morning, and ultimately marries him. The story introduces amongst other historical personages the Earl of Douglas, Lieutenant-General of Scotland; King Robert the Third; the Duke of Albany; and George, Earl of Dunbar and March.

FAIRIES OF POPULAR SUPERSTITION. (1802 *and* 1803)   Po. ii.   254–336

> This essay on elves or fairies forms an introduction to the "Tale of "Tamlane," included among the "Romantic Ballads" in the "Minstrelsy of "the Scottish Border."
>
> Sir W. Scott considerably modified some of the views maintained in this early essay from his pen, in his later-written Letter No. IV. on "Demonology," published in 1830.

FATAL REVENGE; OR, THE FAMILY OF MONTORIO. BY MATURIN, REV. CHARLES ROBERT. (1810)   .   .   .   Pr. xviii.   157

See Maturin.

FIELD OF WATERLOO, THE. (1815)   .   .   .   Po. xi.   255–291

> This was published within four months of the battle of Waterloo, and the profits of the first edition were the author's contribution to the fund raised for the relief of the widows and children of the soldiers slain in the battle. The poem was brought out in a cheap form, and rapidly attained a measure of circulation above what had been reached either by "Rokeby" or "The Lord "of the Isles."

FIELDING, HENRY (1707–1754), MEMOIR OF. (1821–5)   Pr. iii. 77–116.

> This is one of the "Prefaces" in Ballantyne's "Novelist's Library." This life of "the first of British novelists," or, as Lord Byron termed him, "the "prose Homer of human nature," gives a very good running commentary on the principal works of Fielding.
>
> Scott once quoted in a letter a couplet from Fielding's farce "Tumble- "down Dick" which he liked, and he forthwith determined to put it in his "Woodstock" into the mouth of "an old admirer of Shakespeare;" but as Fielding's lines were not written at the period of the novel, he added a note (*see* "Woodstock," Nov. xl. p. 134) that, observing it in Fielding, "it must, as "it was current in the time of the Commonwealth, have reached the author of "'Tom Jones' by tradition; for no one," adds Scott, "will suspect the pres- "ent author of making the anachronism." *See* Lockhart's "Life," vol. viii. pp. 251–52, where is recorded an entry in Scott's diary asserting that he felt assured that it would be easy to swear they were written and that Fielding adopted them from tradition.

FLEETWOOD; OR, THE NEW MAN OF FEELING. BY GODWIN, WIL- LIAM. (1805)   .   .   .   .   .   .   Pr. xviii.   118

See Godwin.

FLY-FISHING, DAYS OF. BY DAVY, SIR HUMPHRY. (1828) Pr. xx.
245.
See Salmonia.

FORESTER'S GUIDE AND PROFITABLE PLANTER, THE. BY MONTEATH,
ROBERT. (1827) . . . . . . Pr. xxi. 1
See Monteath.

FORTUNES OF NIGEL, THE. 2 vols. (1822) . Nov. xxvi. *and* xxvii.

The plot of the story is woven round the Scottish citizen and goldsmith,
George Heriot (1563-1624), who followed James I. to the English capital,
acted as the King's Goldsmith and Banker, and was familiarly called Jingling
Geordie. He was the founder of the well-known Heriot's Hospital for the
education of youth. The romance is laid in London and its vicinity in and
about the year 1620, and an excellent account is given of the liberties of
Alsatia, as Whitefriars was then called.

Among the historical personages introduced are Steenie, the Duke of Buckingham; Charles I., as "Baby Charles;" George Heriot; King James I., and
various heroes and heroines of Alsatia, the sanctuary of outlaws. The story
and notes give much information as to the monstrous murder of Sir Thomas
Overbury by Mrs. Turner, with the connivance of the Duchess of Somerset.
"Nigel" "was considered as ranking in the first class of Scott's romances."

FRAGMENTS, POETICAL . . . . . Po. vi. 373–382
These consist of the "Poacher" and a "Song."

FRANCE, HISTORY OF. 2 vols. (1830) . . Pr. xxvii. *and* xxviii.
See Tales of a Grandfather.

FRANKENSTEIN; OR, THE MODERN PROMETHEUS. (1818) Pr. xviii.
250.

This review appeared in *Blackwood's Edinburgh Magazine* for March,
1818. It is a criticism of Mrs. Shelley's first novel, "A Strange Romance,"
wild and improbable, and esteemed at first a classic; but this early judgment
on its merits has been considerably modified in later years. Scott, when re-
viewing the novel, attributed the authorship to Percy Bysshe Shelley.

FRASER, JAMES BAILLIE (1783–1856): KUZZILBASH, THE: A TALE OF
KHORASAN. (1829) . . . . . Pr. xviii. 393
This review appeared in the *Quarterly* for January, 1829. The romance
was called "Kuzzilbash," which means the "Red-cap," to designate the
Persian soldier, who is so called from that distinguishing part of his uniform.

FROISSART (SIR) JOHN (1337—circa 1400), CHRONICLES OF. BY
    JOHNES, THOMAS. (1805) . . . . Pr. xix. 112

> This review appeared in the *Edinburgh* in January, 1805. The edition
> here reviewed was executed at the Hafod Press, a private printing press
> established by Mr. Johnes (1749-1816) at his superb residence at Hafod.
> His "Froissart," followed by "Monstrelet," are too well known to need
> more than mention.

GALT, JOHN (1779–1839): THE OMEN. (1824) . Pr. xviii. 333

> This review appeared in *Blackwood* for July, 1824. Galt wrote eight or
> ten novels, principally delineating Scottish life and character, but this is not
> considered one of his best.

GEORGE III., KING (1738–1820), MEMOIR OF. (1820) Pr. iv. 322

> This was published in the *Edinburgh Weekly Journal* of February 8, 1820.

GERTRUDE OF WYOMING. BY CAMPBELL, THOMAS. (1809) Pr. xvii.
    267.

> *See* Campbell.

GLOSSARY TO SIR TRISTREM . . Po. v. 463–493

GLOSSARY TO THE WAVERLEY NOVELS . . Nov. xlviii. 431–492

> This is more than a glossary, and contains several interesting old rhymes,
> and so forth. For example, the "Borrowing-days," or the last three days of
> March (O.S.), are described as,—

> > " March borrowed frae Aprile
> > " Three days, an' they were ill;
> > " The first o' them was wind and weet,
> > " The second o' them was snaw and sleet,
> > " The third o' them was sic a freeze
> > " That the birds' legs stack to the trees."

> This rhyme is quoted (see Nov. xii. 230) in Leyden's edition of the "Com-
> "playnt of Scotland."
> Another rhyme worthy of remembrance is,—

> > " Neevie—neevie—nee—nack,
> > " Which hand will you tak,
> > " Tak the right, tak the wrang,
> > " I'll beguile you if I can;"

> which is stated to be a lottery rhyme used among boys while whirling the two
> closed fists round each other,—one containing the prize, the other empty.

GODWIN, WILLIAM (1756–1836): CHAUCER, GEOFFREY, LIFE OF.
(1804) . . . . . . Pr. xvii. 55

This is an article from the *Edinburgh Review* for 1804 on a work by Godwin in two volumes, quarto, upon which the writer says (Lockhart's "Life,"
ii. 177), " I have not either inclination or talents to use the critical scalping
"knife, unless, as in the case of Godwin, where flesh and blood succumbed
"under the temptation." Of this work "on Chaucer," Scott presumed that
the entire edition had been employed by the sapient Government as the
"heaviest materials to be come at" and adopted for blocking up "the mouth
"of our enemy's harbours." The scalping-knife is amusingly used where
(p. 69) he corrects Mr. Godwin, who had blamed Chaucer for "polluting the
"portrait of Creseide's virgin character in the beginning of the poem with so
"low and pitiful joke as this:

> " ' But whether that she children had, or none,
> " ' I rede it not, therefore I let it gone.' "

In which lines (as Scott says) Chaucer intended no joke, inasmuch as Creseide was a young widow:

> " And as a widowe was she and alone."

Nor does the critic consider it other than a "poor excuse" (p. 70), "after
"writing a huge book, to tell the reader that it is but ' superficial work' be-
"cause the author came a novice to such an undertaking." Ile advises Mr.
Godwin in future "to read before he writes, and not merely while he is
"writing." The whole may be characterized as a "slashing review."

Godwin could not properly have made a work of many pages, much less
two volumes, on the life of Chaucer, so he padded it with "memoirs of his
"[Chaucer's] near friend and kinsman, John of Gaunt, Duke of Lancaster,
"[and] with sketches of the manners, opinions, arts, and literature of England
"in the fourteenth century."

GODWIN, WILLIAM: FLEETWOOD; OR, THE NEW MAN OF FEELING.
(1805) . . . . . . Pr. xviii. 118

This appeared in the *Edinburgh Review* for 1805. It is an outline of the
novel, and closes with some reasons for objecting to such a "Man of Feel-
"ing" as the despicable hero of this book.

GOETZ OF BERLICHINGEN: A TRAGEDY. (1799) . Po. xii. 443

Monk Lewis negotiated the sale of Scott's version of Goethe's tragedy
for £26.5.0, with a further payment of a like sum in case of a second edition, but "none was called for until long after the copyright had expired."
Goetz was a real character, and was called Iron Hand, having lost his right
hand for contravening an ordinance of Maximilian, the grandfather of Charles
V., published in 1495, against duelling. "A machine," it is related, "was
"made and fitted to his right arm, whence he was called ' Iron Hand.' "

GOLDSMITH, OLIVER (1728–1774), MEMOIR OF. (1821–5) Pr. iii. 231.

This is one of the " Prefaces" in Ballantyne's " Novelist's Library." This charming sketch gives too brief an account of one " who touched nothing " that he did not adorn," as Dr. Johnson affirmed in the epitaph placed in Westminster Abbey to Goldsmith's memory. It touches lightly on his acting as a " reader" in the printing-house of Samuel Richardson, and the well known anecdote of Dr. Johnson's selling for him the " Vicar of Wakefield" for £60 when Goldsmith was in trouble with his landlady on account of overdue rent. It gives many a sample of his habits of forgetfulness, as, for instance, when he sallied forth from some apartments he had engaged, he forgot to ask the name or address of the landlady, and could never have returned " had he not met the porter who had carried his luggage."

This forgetfulness served him in good stead at times, for once when he was going to Leyden, forgetting about his destination, he embarked in a ship which was bound from Leith for Bordeaux, and was fortunately driven into Newcastle-upon-Tyne by stress of weather, where he succeeded in getting locked up in a prison, and on his release found that his ship had sailed. It was wrecked at the mouth of the Garonne, and every soul on board perished.

His comedy of the "Good-Natured Man" (1768) ran nine nights. His " She Stoops to Conquer" still retains a place on the stage. The main incident in the latter play, of mistaking a gentleman's residence for an inn, was borrowed from a blunder of the author himself while travelling in Ireland.

GUY MANNERING; OR, THE ASTROLOGER. 2 vols. (1815) Nov. iii. *and* iv.

This was received with eager curiosity, and pronounced by acclamation fully worthy to share the honours of " Waverley." In the spring of 1816, Daniel Terry, the actor (1780–1828), produced a dramatic version of this novel "which met with great success on the London boards, and still con-"tinues to be a favourite with the theatrical public." The novel was published " exactly two months after the ' Lord of the Isles' was dismissed from " the author's desk." In Lockhart's " Life" (vol. v. pp. 397–408) is given the ballad from " The Durham Garland," recovered "after Sir W. Scott's "death," which "in fact contains a great deal more of the main fable" of " Guy Mannering" "than the other versions mentioned by the author in his " Introduction." He probably had read it in his boyhood and remembered the purport of it, though its actual words could not just at the time be recalled.— *See* Lockhart's " Life" (vol. v. pp. 5 and 35, 36).

The principal incidents of this story are founded on facts. The two characters which live most actively in the memory undoubtedly are " Dominie "Sampson, the stickit minister" and eccentric schoolmaster with a "pro-di-"gi-ous" amount of unapplied learning; and Meg Merrilies, whose personality has been graven on the mind even more deeply than in the novel by the superb acting of Miss Charlotte Cushman. The gipsy on whom the character of Meg was founded was well known in the middle of the eighteenth century "by the name of Jean Gordon, an inhabitant of the village of "Kirk Yetholm, in the Cheviot Hills, adjoining the English border." The author adds (Nov. iii. p. 23), "Such a preceptor as Mr. Sampson is supposed "to have been was actually tutor in the family of a gentleman of consider- "able property." The events of the tale are laid in the years 1750-70, in the reigns of George II. and George III.

Andrew Crosby, whose portrait hangs in the Parliament Hall, Edinburgh, was the original of the shrewd and witty Counsellor Pleydell.

HAJJI BABA OF ISPAHAN IN ENGLAND. BY MORIER, JAMES. (1829)
Pr. xviii. 354

See Morier.

HALIDON HILL. (1822) . . . . . . Po. xii. 1-86

This is a "Dramatic Sketch from Scottish History." Halidon Hill is situ- ate about two miles northwest of Berwick-on-Tweed, England, where, July 19, 1333, the English under Edward III. defeated the Scots under the Re- gent Archibald Douglas. The scene utilized by Scott was really Homildon Hill, a height near Wooler in Northumberland, England, where the English under Percy defeated the Scots under Douglas in 1402. The Regent of the play is a purely imaginary character.

Messrs. Constable, without seeing the manuscript, offered £1000 for the copyright, which was accepted. Scott did not succeed in dramatic composi- tion. Whether he could have done so if he had taken the necessary care and pains is not to the point. His dramatic pieces "would have been long "since forgotten, but that they came from Scott's pen."

HAROLD THE DAUNTLESS. (1817) . . . Po. xi. 143-254

This was published "by the author of the 'Bridal of Triermain'" within less than a month of the publication of "The Black Dwarf" and "Old "Mortality." A sketch of it had been actually printed in 1809 in the *Edinburgh Annual Register*, avowedly as one of three imitations of "Living "Poets." The comparative failure of this piece resolved Sir Walter that he would "never again adventure in poetry on a grand scale." Scott's own feeling was that "it turned vapid upon his imagination, and he had finished "it at last with hurry and impatience."

Again the critics were on a false scent, and the *Critical Review* styled "Harold" "a tolerably successful imitation of some parts of the style of Mr. "Walter Scott, but, like all imitations, it is clearly distinguishable from the "prototype: it wants the life and seasoning of originality." *Blackwood's* criticism on it (*see* Po. xi. pp. 252-254) describes it as "one of the closest "and most successful imitations," without being either "a caricature or a "parody, that perhaps ever appeared in any language." This makes amusing reading. In three or four years it was found to be Sir W. Scott's own work.

HEART OF MIDLOTHIAN, THE. 2 vols. (1818) Nov. xi., 139–419;
    xii. *and* xiii., 1–234.

This formed the second series of the "Tales of My Landlord." The
events are laid in the years 1736-51, in the reign of George II., and gather
round the noisy scenes of the Porteous Riot in Edinburgh. Porteous was
captain of the Edinburgh City Guard, and fired upon the people for a dis-
turbance made when a noted smuggler named Wilson was hanged. Porteous
was tried for shooting the people illegally, and was himself sentenced to be
hanged; but the people, believing the sentence would not be carried into effect,
broke into the prison while Porteous was rejoicing with friends at an antici-
pated speedy reprieve, and executed him. The character of Jeanie Deans,
the heroine of the story, had a real prototype in the person of Helen Walker, who walked to London to ask and obtained the pardon of her sister,
who was under sentence of death for child murder. They were the daughters
of a small farmer in a place called Dalwhairn, in the parish of Irongray,
Dumfriesshire. The historical personages, the Duke of Argyle, Queen Caro-
line the consort of George II., Porteous, Lady Suffolk, and others, and the
strongly marked characters of Madge Wildfire and the grand Jeanie Deans,
lend this story extreme interest. The "Heart of Midlothian" was a name
given to the old jail or Tolbooth of Edinburgh. It was taken down in 1817.
Sir Walter Scott caused a monument to be erected over the grave of Helen
Walker to her memory. The novelist gives (vol. xi. pp. 151*–152*) several
particulars of Helen and Isabella Walker, the latter of whom, after being
saved by her sister, was married to the person (named Waugh) who had
wronged her, and "lived happily for great part of a century, uniformly
"acknowledging the extraordinary affection to which she owed her preser-
"vation." Helen was never married. In vol. xiii. at pp. 36–39 are some
interesting particulars of Madge Wildfire.

HERBERT, THE HONOURABLE AND REV. WILLIAM (1778–1847):
    HERBERT'S POEMS. (1806) . . . Pr. xvii. 102

This was a review published in the *Edinburgh Review* for 1806 upon two
volumes of "Miscellaneous Poetry" by Mr. Herbert.

The way in which the celebrated "Death Song of Regnar Lodbrog" had
become perverted, and the exact contrary of the original had been given in
English versions of Scaldic poetry by reason of being translated from Icelandic into Latin and thence into English, is amusingly shown (p. 104) by apt
quotations. Mr. Herbert translated directly from the Icelandic, and so cor-
rected many gross blunders.

HIGHLAND WIDOW, THE. (1827) . . . Nov. xli. 121–237

This tale, laid in the year 1755, in the reign of George II., was derived from
the author's friend, Mrs. Murray Keith. "Neither the Highland cicerone
"MacLeish, nor the demure waiting-woman, were drawn from imagination."
The tale is related "very much as the excellent old lady used to tell the
"story," and forms the first of the first series of "Tales of the Canongate."

SIR WALTER SCOTT'S WRITINGS

HOFFMANN, ERNEST THEODORE WILLIAM (1776–1822), NOVELS OF. (1827) . . . . . . Pr. xviii. 270

Hoffmann's third name is variously given as William, Wolfgang, and Amadeus. This review appeared in the first number of the *Foreign Quarterly* for July, 1827. It gives a very interesting account of the author, whose career was both painful and extraordinary. He was one of the "most remarkable and "original of German story tellers." Carlyle, in 1827, wrote an interesting account of him, now included in his "Critical and Miscellaneous Essays." Hoffmann led an extremely ill-regulated life, and when success had turned his head, he, in disgust with conventionalities, retired to the wine house. "Strangers," says one of his biographers, "came to Berlin to see him in the "tavern. The tavern was his study, his pulpit, and his throne. Here his wit "flashed and flamed like an aurora borealis, and the table was forever in a "roar; and thus, amid tobacco smoke and over coarse earthly liquor, was Hoff- "mann, wasting faculties which might have seasoned the nectar of the gods." His personal courage and literary industry in the last painful years of his life, when suffering a medical martyrdom, are a curious warning how "the most "fertile fancy may be exhausted by the lavish prodigality of its possessor." The three novels criticised by Scott are Hoffmann's "Leben und Nachlass" (1823), "Serapions-Brüder" (1819–26), and "Nachtstücke" (1816).

HOME, JOHN (1724–1808), LIFE AND WORKS OF. BY MACKENZIE, HENRY. (1827) . . . . . . Pr. xix. 283

This long article appeared in the *Quarterly* for June, 1827. Scott met the author of "Douglas" at Bath, when Home was still a young man, and retained many later kindly recollections of him. In writing of this review in his "Diary," Scott says: "Home's works are poorer than I thought them: "good blank verse and stately sentiment, but something lukewarmish, except- "ing Douglas, which is certainly a masterpiece; even that does not stand the "closet. Its merits are for the stage; and it is certainly one of the best act- "ing plays going." He adds, "I finished the criticism on Home, adding a "string of Jacobite anecdotes, like that which boys put to a kite's tail."

HOUSE OF ASPEN, THE: A TRAGEDY. (1799) . Po. xii. 363–441

This is a very free "translation from one of the minor dramatists," executed by Scott in 1799, but first published in "The Keepsake" of 1829, "one of "the literary almanacks." Sir W. Scott received £500 for permission to print this with "My Aunt Margaret's Mirror," "The Tapestried Chamber," and "The Death of the Laird's Jock" in "The Keepsake," but regretted "having "meddled in any way with the toy-shop of literature, and would never do "so again, though repeatedly offered very large sums." (*See* Life ii. 19, *and* ix. 208.)

HUDSON, MRS., AND DONAT, MRS.: COOKERY, NEW PRACTICE OF.
   (1805) . . . . Pr. xix. 100
   See Cookery.

HUNTER, DR. A. COOKERY, RECEIPTS IN MODERN. (1805) Pr.
   xix. 107.
   See Cookery.

IGNOTUS: COOKERY, RECEIPTS IN MODERN. (1805) Pr. xix. 107
   See Cookery.

IMITATIONS OF THE ANCIENT BALLAD. BY MODERN AUTHORS. Po. iv.
   89–388.
   See Minstrelsy of the Scottish Border.

IMITATIONS OF THE ANCIENT BALLAD, ESSAY ON. (1830) Po. iv. 3–87
   See Ballad.

INDEX TO MEMOIRS OF THE LIFE OF SIR WALTER SCOTT. L. x.
   277–359.

INDEX TO MISCELLANEOUS WORKS . . Pr. xxviii. 283–363

INDEX TO POETICAL WORKS . . Po. xii. 563–593

INDEX TO PUBLICATIONS OF SIR WALTER SCOTT. . L. x. 269–276
   See Chronological List.

INDEXES.
   See Chronological List *and* Glossary.

IVANHOE. 2 vols. (1819) . . . . Nov. xvi. *and* xvii.

   The events of this story are laid as far back as 1194, in the time of Richard
   I., and apart from the leading interest in such quotable characters as Rebecca
   and Ivanhoe, Isaac the Jew and Lady Rowena, who does not revel in the
   tournaments, feudal life, and attractions developed in this story of the Cœur
   de Lion, Robin Hood, Allan-a-Dale, Friar Tuck, and the treacherous John,
   the brother and successor of Richard? The publication of "Ivanhoe" marks
   the most brilliant epoch in Scott's history as the "literary favourite of his
   "contemporaries." This was Scott's first departure from writing "Scottish
   "novels." He had a perfect fascination, apparently, for writing anonymously, and proposed to do so in this instance, but his publishers knew better,

and as a compromise it was published "by the Author of Waverley." He went to see "Ivanhoe" at the Odéon in Paris, and records that it was strange to hear anything like the words which he "then in agony of pain with spasms "in his stomach" dictated to William Laidlaw, at Abbotsford, recited in a foreign tongue and for the amusement of a strange people. "I little thought," he adds, "to have survived the completing of this novel." This and the two novels—"The Bride of Lammermoor" and "The Legend of Montrose"— were all written by dictation "through fits of agonizing cramp of the stomach "so acute that Scott could not suppress cries of agony."

A fac-simile of a page of the original manuscript of "Ivanhoe" is given in Lockhart's "Life" (vol. vi. p. 175).

JOHN DE LANCASTER : A NOVEL. BY CUMBERLAND, RICHARD. (1809)
Pr. xviii. 138

See Cumberland.

JOHNES, THOMAS (1748–1816): FROISSART, (SIR) JOHN, CHRONICLES OF. (1805) . . . . . . Pr. xix. 112

See Froissart.

JOHNSON, SAMUEL (1709–1783), MEMOIR OF. (1821–5) Pr. iii. 260

This is one of the "Prefaces" in Ballantyne's "Novelist's Library." So many anecdotes of the rough manners of this honour to literature have gone the rounds, that it is happy to recall the saying of Oliver Goldsmith, who knew him well: "Johnson, to be sure, has a roughness in his manner, but no man "alive has a more tender heart. He has nothing of the bear but his skin." Sir Walter Scott used to declare (*see* Lockhart's "Life," vol. iii. p. 269) that he "had more pleasure in reading 'London' and 'The Vanity of Human "'Wishes' than any other poetical composition he could mention." The last line of manuscript that Scott sent to the press was a quotation from the latter poem.

JOHNSTONE, CHARLES (1720–1800), MEMOIR OF. (1821–5) Pr. iii. 427.

This is one of the "Prefaces" in Ballantyne's "Novelist's Library." Johnstone is practically only known as the author of the book "Chrysal; or, The "Adventures of a Guinea," which is an exposure of the personal and secret history of then living characters, written in imitation of Le Sage's "Devil "on Two Sticks," and aptly described by Dr. Chalmers as "the best scandalous "chronicle of the day." A key to the personages was actually supplied by the author himself to two friends, and it has been published by William Davis in his collection of "Bibliographical and Literary Anecdotes." It was re-printed in Ballantyne's edition, for which Scott wrote this Preface.

KELLY, MICHAEL (1762–1826), REMINISCENCES OF. (1826) Pr. xx.
233.

This review appeared in the *Quarterly* for April, 1826. The laborious
way in which Sheridan's "School for Scandal" was written, and the several
sketches altered and polished till the superb comedy was evolved, is well
known. By way of contrast, Kelly relates (p. 241) that all of the fifth act of
"Pizarro" (a translation from Kotzebue) was not actually written when the
first night of the new play arrived, and that Sheridan was writing the last
part of the play whilst the earlier parts were acting. The review of Kelly
the composer is enhanced by the necessary intermingling of extraordinary
anecdotes of Kelly's partner and companion, the celebrated and eccentric
Sheridan. The tricks of the latter on Kelly were innumerable, and Sheridan
"vouches" that Kelly's truest Irish blood showed itself when, having received
a dangerous fall on the stage, he exclaimed, "And if I had been killed now,
"who was to maintain me for the rest of my life."

KEMBLE, JOHN PHILIP (1757–1823), MEMOIRS OF THE LIFE OF. BY
BOADEN, JAMES. (1826) . . . . Pr. xx. 152

This review appeared in the *Quarterly* for April, 1826. Kemble's theatrical career extended, subject to some minor appearances at ten years of
age, from 1776 to 1817. The Kembles, including Mrs. Siddons, their sister,
formed a mighty power on the stage, and Sir Walter has given a pleasant
review of John Philip, with whom and Mrs. Siddons he was on terms of considerable friendship. The review has many bright anecdotes. Mrs. Siddons,
we are told by Lockhart in a note (Lockhart's "Life," vol. iii. p. 214), often,
in familiar table-talk, fell into the use of blank verse, and "Scott (who was a
"capital mimic) often repeated her tragic exclamation to a footboy during a
"dinner at Ashestiel,—

"'You've brought me water, boy,—I asked for beer.'"

KENILWORTH. 2 vols. (1821) . . . Nov. xxii. *and* xxiii.

The success of "The Abbot" and the reception accorded to the story of
"Mary, Queen of Scots," made the author desire to bring "her sister and
"foe," Elizabeth, into a tale. Constable, the publisher, pressed him to write
of the period and subject of "The Armada;" but whilst Scott comforted him
by promising to write of Elizabeth, he decided with himself to revert to an
old ballad story, entitled "Cumnor Hall," which he had stored in his memory
for many long years. He even wanted to call the novel by the same name as
the ballad, but was dissuaded by Constable, who suggested "Kenilworth,"
and carried his point against the opinion of John Ballantyne, who told Constable that the tale if named "Kenilworth" would "result in its being some-
"thing worthy of a kennel." Ballantyne was wrong, and Mr. Cadell relates
that Constable's vanity boiled over so much on having his suggestion adopted,

that, in his high moods, he used to stalk up and down his room with his hands beneath his coat-tails, exclaiming, " By Jove! I am all but the author of the " Waverley Novels."

The ballad of " Cumnor Hall," by William Julius Mickle (1734-1788), is to be found in Evans's " Ancient Ballads" (vol. iv, p. 130), and a copy is given in Nov. xxii. pp. xii.-xv.

The pathetic and tragical story of " Amy Robsart," and the long list of historical personages and scenes introduced, including Lord Burleigh, the Earl of Leicester, Elizabeth, Walter Raleigh, Shakespeare, the Earl of Sussex, and Richard Varney, swept his novel into the full tide of instantaneous success. The events are laid in 1575, in the time of Elizabeth.

A ground plan of Kenilworth Castle is given at the beginning of Nov. xxiii. When now visiting the scanty ruins, which are all that remain of the pile so ruthlessly destroyed by Cromwell, it seems incredible that in its glory, some two hundred and twenty-five years ago only, it could have been the magnificent pile described by Scott.

This review appeared in the *Quarterly* for January, 1818. Kirkton's " Secret and True History of the Church of Scotland" was edited by Mr. Charles Kirkpatrick Sharpe from the original manuscript. It only embraces the period between the Restoration and the year 1678, when Kirkton was compelled to fly to Holland. Mr. Sharpe has printed, as an addition, the account of the murder of Archbishop Sharp by James Russell, one of the actors.

See Fraser.

For the copyright of this poem the author received £2100, and down to July, 1836, "the legitimate sale in Great Britain was not less than fifty thou-"sand copies." The critics were in " full harmony with each other and with "the popular voice." The review in the *Quarterly* was written by George Ellis, that in the *Edinburgh* by Jeffrey.

It has been well stated that of Scott's principal poems "' The Lay of the "' Last Minstrel' is generally considered the most natural and original, "' Marmion' as the most powerful and splendid, and ' The Lady of the Lake' "as the most interesting, romantic, picturesque, and graceful," as also it is undoubtedly the most read.

It is a perfect guide-book to the fairy scene of the Trosachs and Loch Katrine in the Western Highlands of Perthshire.

James Ballantyne records in his " Memorandum" the incident of finding

Miss Scott (then quite young) in Sir Walter Scott's library, shortly after the publication of "The Lady of the Lake," when he asked her, "Well, Miss "Sophia, how do you like 'The Lady of the Lake'?" but received the unexpected answer, given with perfect simplicity, "Oh, I have not read it; papa "says there's nothing so bad for young people as reading bad poetry."

LANDSCAPE GARDENING [PLANTER'S GUIDE]. (1828) Pr. xxi. 77
See Steuart, Sir Henry.

LAY OF THE LAST MINSTREL, THE. (1805) . . Po. vi. 1-288

This was the stepping-stone to Sir Walter Scott's great fame. It met with the approval of William Pitt, Charles Fox, and of such critics as Lord Jeffrey, and upwards of forty-four thousand copies were disposed of by the trade before Sir Walter superintended the edition of 1830, to which his biographical introductions were prefixed. He received £169.6.0 as a share of profits and £500 for the copyright, to which the publishers "added £100 in their own "unsolicited kindness." The date of the tale is about the middle of the sixteenth century. It was written "at about the rate of a canto per week. "There was, indeed, little occasion for pause or hesitation, when a trouble-"some rhyme might be accommodated by an alteration of the stanza, or where "an incorrect measure might be remedied by a variation in the rhyme." The original manuscript has not been preserved.

LEBEN UND NACHLASS. BY HOFFMANN, ERNEST THEODORE WILLIAM . . . . Pr. xviii. 270
See Hoffmann.

LEGEND OF MONTROSE, A. (1819) . . . . . Nov. xv.

This with the "Bride of Lammermoor" formed the third series of "Tales "of My Landlord." The scene is laid in 1645-46, in the reign of Charles I., and was "written chiefly with a view to place before the reader the melan-"choly fate of John, Lord Kilpont, eldest son of William, Earl of Airth and "Menteith, and the singular circumstances attending the birth and history of "James Stewart, of Ardvoirlich, by whose hands the unfortunate nobleman" fell, about 1644. The character of Dugald Dalgetty, the soldier of fortune, ranks as a companion picture with the inimitable Bailie Nicol Jarvie. Dalgetty had a prototype in Colonel Robert Monro, who was a member of the Scottish regiment called MacKeyes' regiment, of which he published a history in 1637, describing the expedition with "the worthy Scots Regiment "(called MacKeyes' Regiment) levied in August 1626 and reduced after "the Battaile of Nerling to one Company in September 1634 at Wormes in "the Paltz. To which is annexed the Abridgement of Exercise &c." London. 1637. Folio.

A "correct version" of the slaughter of Lord Kilpont, furnished to Sir W.

Scott while the novel "was passing through the press" by Robert Stewart of Ardvoirlich, a descendant of the James Stewart of the legend, is given, pp. 25-31.

Among the historical characters introduced into the novel are: McCallum More the Marquis of Argyle, the Lord Justice General of Scotland, and the Marquis of Montrose.

LENORE: TRANSLATION FROM BÜRGER. (1795) . Po. vi. 291

This translation or "imitation from 'Lenore'" was written with the title "William and Helen." It is of great interest, as being among the earliest of Sir Walter's writings, excluding, of course, his school and college efforts. He made a rhymed translation of this in one evening, "beginning his task "after supper and not retiring to bed until he had finished it, having by this "time worked himself into a state of excitement which set sleep at defiance." The translation was published in October, 1796, with that of "The Wild "Huntsman," also from Bürger, in a thin quarto, "by the request of friends," without any author's name on the title-page. The venture was not pecuni-arily successful, and many copies were consigned to the waste-paper trunk. (*See* Po. iv. 55-63.)

LE SAGE, ALAIN RENÉ (1668-1747), MEMOIR OF. (1821-5) Pr. iii. 390.

This is one of the "Prefaces" in Ballantyne's "Novelist's Library." Le Sage was a bold and independent man. He was urged to "read" a play before the Duchess of Bouillon, but was unavoidably detained in a law court, and so reached his appointment two hours late. The Duchess received his apology with coldness, and added that he had made the company lose two hours in waiting for his arrival, to which he retorted, "It is easy to make up the loss, "madame; I will not read my comedy, and you will thus regain the lost time." Without hesitation he left the hotel, and could never be prevailed on to return thither. So when he wrote his celebrated play "Turcaret," which exposed the iniquities of the agents of the revenue, he was offered one hundred thou-sand francs to suppress the piece, but refused the bribe, and the piece was played and proved successful in spite of the cabal raised against it.

His "Devil on Two Sticks" and "Gil Blas" will last as long as literature lasts.

LEYDEN, JOHN, M.D. (1775-1811), MEMOIRS OF. (1811) Pr. iv. 137.

This was first published in volume iv. of the *Edinburgh Annual Register.* Sir Walter Scott was very much attached to this remarkable man, whom he never named "but with an expression of regard and a moistening eye." Dr. Leyden was loud and uncouth in manners, with a voice described as "saw-"tones," and accustomed to breathe the "threats of a lion, but possessed of the "heart of a lamb." He was a man of astonishing erudition, and was trained for a minister of the Church of Scotland, but took to medicine, and entered the service of the East India Company. He acquired the Sanscrit, Persian, Hindostanee, and other Asiatic languages, and among his other literary efforts contributed to the " Minstrelsy of the Scottish Border."

LOCKHART, JOHN GIBSON : SCOTT, SIR WALTER, MEMOIRS OF. 10 vols.
(1836) . . . . L. i.-x.
See Scott.

LORD OF ENNERDALE, THE . . . . Nov. i., lv.-lxiv.

This is a fragment of an "attempt at a tale . . . which was almost in- " stantly abandoned."

LORD OF THE ISLES, THE. (1815) . . . . Po. x. 1-352

With this Sir Walter decided " to close his poetic labours upon an extended " scale." The sale would have been regarded by most authors a splendid success. Before his poetical works were collected, twelve thousand two hundred and fifty copies were sold; but the success of " Waverley" and the phenomenal sales of Lord Byron's works at that time convinced him that "since one line had failed he must stick to something else," and in less than two months he published " Guy Mannering." Sir Walter Scott in 1830 wrote of this poem, " The sale of fifteen thousand copies enabled the author to " retreat from the field of poetry with the honours of war."

The story opens in the spring of the year 1307, and many of the personages and incidents introduced are (says the author) of historical celebrity.

MACDUFF'S CROSS. (1822) . . . . . Po. xii. 87-111

This first appeared in Joanna Baillie's "Collection of Poetical Miscel- " lanies," published in 1823. It is a dramatic sketch about the Cross, which was " a place of refuge to any person related to MacDuff within the ninth " degree who, having committed a homicide in sudden quarrel, should reach " this place, prove his descent from the Thane of Fife, and pay a certain " penalty." The shaft of the Cross was destroyed at the Reformation in 1559.

The right of sanctuary was granted to the MacDuff of Shakespeare's " Macbeth" for the service he rendered in overthrowing that usurper at the battle of Lumphanan, in Aberdeenshire, August 15, 1057.

MACKENZIE, HENRY (1745-1831): HOME, JOHN, THE LIFE AND
WORKS OF. (1827) . . . . . Pr. xix. 283
See Home.

MACKENZIE, HENRY, MEMOIR OF. (1821-5) . . Pr. iv. 1

This is one of the " Prefaces" in Ballantyne's " Novelist's Library." The author published " The Man of Feeling" anonymously in 1771, and was successful both in poetry and the drama. He was also the editor of the *Mirror* and the *Lounger*, two of the periodicals based on the foundation of the *Tatler*, etc.

The success of the anonymous "Man of Feeling" led a Mr. Eccles, a young clergyman of Bath, to lay claim to its authorship. He transcribed the whole in his own hand, with blottings, interlineations, and corrections. He maintained his assumed right with such plausible pertinacity that Messrs. Cadell and Strachan (Mr. Mackenzie's publishers) found it necessary to un-deceive the public by a formal contradiction. Mr. Eccles was drowned in the Avon whilst bathing, and the *Gentleman's Magazine* for September, 1777, gave an epitaph on this literary impostor, commencing—

" Beneath this stone ' The Man of Feeling' lies——"

MALAGROWTHER, MALACHI: LETTERS TO THE EDITOR OF THE EDIN-
BURGH WEEKLY JOURNAL ON THE PROPOSED CHANGE OF
CURRENCY AND OTHER LATE ALTERATIONS, AS THEY AF-
FECT OR ARE INTENDED TO AFFECT, THE KINGDOM OF SCOT-
LAND. (1826) . . . . . . Pr. xxi. 267-402

These three letters were addressed to the author's friend, James Ballantyne, the editor of the *Edinburgh Weekly Journal*, and they appeared in that newspaper in February and March, 1826. They were much discussed, and were answered by the then Secretary of the Admiralty, Mr. Croker, but the proposed measure, as regarded Scotland, was ultimately abandoned—and that result was universally ascribed to Malachi Malagrowther. The dispute was whether a measure proposed for England should be extended to Scotland, whereby private banks were to be restricted from issuing their own notes as money and limiting the Bank of England to the issue of notes of £5 value and upwards.

MARMION: A TALE OF FLODDEN-FIELD. (1808) . . Po. vii.

The poem opens about the commencement of August, 1513, and closes with the defeat of the Scots under James IV. by the English under the Earl of Surrey on September 9 of the same year. The king and many of the nobles were among the slain. The hero is a fictitious character.

This was reviewed by Jeffrey in the *Edinburgh Review* for April, 1808, with all that critic's able but disagreeable severity. Different opinions on politics and a sense of injury at Jeffrey's hands as a reviewer led to a final separation of Scott from the *Edinburgh*. Jeffrey himself sent a copy of the review to Scott, and dined at the poet's table a few days later, when Mrs. Scott showed more feeling than her husband had done, for when her guest

was departing she said, " Well, good-night, Mr. Jeffrey. Dey tell me you
" have abused Scott in de *Review*, and I hope Mr. Constable has paid you
" very well for writing it." Sir Walter was paid £1050 for this poem by
Constable " very shortly after it was begun, and before he had seen a line of
" it." As many as fifty thousand copies of this poem were sold before " Mar-
" mion" was included in the first collective edition of Scott's " Poetical
" Works."

The introductions to the several cantos assume the form of familiar epistles
to intimate friends.

Lord Byron included Scott and " Marmion" in his " English Bards and
" Scotch Reviewers."

> " And think'st thou, Scott ! by vain conceit, perchance,
> " On public taste to foist thy stale romance,
> " Though Murray with his Miller may combine
> " To yield thy muse just half-a-crown per line?
> " No ! when the sons of song descend to trade
> " Their bays are sere, their former laurels fade.
> " Let such forego the poet's sacred name,
> " Who rack their brains for lucre, not for fame."

This, with more in the same strain, is pretty tolerable fustian from an author
who received £15,455 from the same Mr. Murray for his own " song" sold
to the " trade."

By way of frontispiece this volume has a copy of J. M. W. Turner's view
of Edinburgh.

A fac-simile of a stanza of the poem is given between pp. 218–219.

MATURIN, REV. CHARLES ROBERT (1782–1824): FATAL REVENGE; OR,
THE FAMILY OF MONTORIO (1810) . . Pr. xviii. 157

This review appeared in the *Quarterly* of 1810. The " Fatal Revenge"
was Maturin's first novel, and was " written in a terrific and gloomy style, after
" the manner of Monk Lewis, displaying some genius and much bombast, and
" strongly dashed with the mysterious colouring of the Castle of Udolpho"
in Mrs. Radcliffe's novel, " The Mysteries of Udolpho." Both Byron and
Scott greatly befriended Maturin. The novel was published under the *nom
de plume* of Dennis Jasper Murphy.

MATURIN, REV. CHARLES ROBERT: WOMEN; OR, POUR ET CONTRE.
(1818) . . . . Pr. xviii. 172

Mr. Maturin was an Irishman to the backbone—always in hopes, and un-
crushed even by the pursuit of bailiffs. He was an eccentric, and when he
sent his play of " Bertram" to Lord Byron asking him to assist him in getting
it produced, he sent no address, and Lord Byron had great trouble to find the
author. When the " fitt" of composition was on him he used to place a wafer
on his forehead, and the family might not then address him till the " fitt" was
off. This review appeared in the *Edinburgh* of 1818.

METRICAL ROMANCES, ANCIENT ENGLISH, SELECTED BY JOSEPH RIT-
SON. (1806) . . . . . . Pr. xvii. 16
See Ritson.

METRICAL ROMANCES, SPECIMENS OF EARLY ENGLISH. (1806) Pr.
xvii. 16.
See Ellis.

MINSTRELSY OF THE SCOTTISH BORDER. (Introduction dated 1802–
1803) . . . . Po. i. 92–291

This formed the original essay prefixed to the " Minstrelsy of the Scottish
" Border," as published in 1802.

According to Mr. Motherwell, the editor of " Minstrelsy Ancient and
" Modern, 1827," the old ballads which appeared for the first time in Scott's
collection were forty-three in number. A list of these is given, Po. i. pp.
v., vi.

In the advertisement to the " Minstrelsy" (Po. i. pp. 3–8), the writer, Mr. J.
G. Lockhart, points out that " in the text and notes of this early publication we
" can now [1833] trace the primary incident or broad outline of almost every
" romance, whether in verse or in prose, which Sir Walter Scott built in after
" life on the history or traditions of his country."

MINSTRELSY OF THE SCOTTISH BORDER. 4 vols. (1802 *and* 1803)
Po. i. 293–428, ii., iii., *and* iv.

The history of Scott's " Minstrelsy" was a checkered one. The first edition
in 1802 of volumes i. and ii. consisted of eight hundred and fifty copies, but
his one-half share of the clear profits amounted only to £78.10. Volume iii.
was published in 1803, and before 1820 five further editions of five thousand
five hundred copies had been published, and he had received £500 for the
copyright.

The " Minstrelsy" contains three classes of poems: I. Historical Ballads;
II. Romantic Ballads; III. Imitations of the Ancient Ballad by modern
authors. The majority of the ballads are accompanied by elaborate accounts
of their history and evolution, written by Sir W. Scott. Ten of the ballads
are accompanied by the airs which are appended in this edition, being those
which Sir W. Scott liked best. " They are transcribed without variation
" from the manuscripts in his library." The ten old ballads so distinguished
are:

BATTLE OF BOTHWELL BRIGG . . . . . Po. ii.	247
BATTLE OF OTTERBURN . . . . . Po. i.	369
DICK O' THE COW . . . . . . Po. ii.	63
DOUGLAS TRAGEDY . . . . . . Po. iii.	1
DOWIE DENS O' YARROW . . . . . Po. iii.	151
GLENFINLAS . . . . . . Po. iv.	169

The imitations by Sir W. Scott himself are:

This selection consists of the fifteen pieces enumerated below:

This was written under the threat of invasion in the autumn of 1804, and was published in the "English "Minstrelsy."

First appeared in the *Edinburgh Annual Register* for 1809. It was designed for a monument in Lichfield Cathedral, at the burial-place of the family of Miss Seward.

This was a prologue to Miss Baillie's play of this name produced at Edinburgh in 1809-10. The prologue was spoken by the author's friend, Mr. Daniel Terry.

This is a translation from the Gaelic.

This first appeared in the *Edinburgh Annual Register* for 1808, and in 1817 was set to a Welsh air in vol. iii. of Thomson's "Select Melodies."

It does not seem clear where this was first published.

Published in Haydn's "Collection of Scottish Airs," vol. ii.

This was published in the *Edinburgh Review* for October, 1806. Lockhart styles it an "exquisite piece of humour." The cited extracts point to this work being a book full of fun. Among the "school miseries" is included "seeing the boy who is next above you flogged for a repetition, which "you know you cannot say half so well as he did." He concludes the article with a series of suggested "Reviewer's Groans," which were mainly suggested by Lord Jeffrey, and are offered as a thankoffering for pleasant reading, but hinting how heavy are the sorrows of the critic who wades through good, bad, and indifferent volumes to extract subject for an article, and frequently closes the hide-bound transgressor "with the fruitless apos-"trophe,—

"'Too bad for a blessing, too good for a curse,
"'I wish from my soul thou wert better or worse.'"

MOLIÈRE [JEAN BAPTISTE POQUELIN, *called*] (1622–1673). Pr. xvii.
137.

This is a review published in the *Foreign Quarterly Review* for 1828 on
Auger's edition of "Molière," in nine volumes, published in Paris, 1819–27,
and on Taschereau's " Histoire de la Vie et des Ouvrages de Molière."

It gives an excellent epitome, vivaciously written, of the long series of
works produced by the "prince of the writers of comedy."

MONASTERY, THE. 2 vols. (1820) . . . Nov. xviii. *and* xix.

The celebrated ruins of Melrose Abbey are the scene designated in the
romance as the " Monastery of St. Mary's of Kennaquhair and its depend-
" encies." The events are laid in 1559, etc., in the time of Queen Elizabeth,
and among the historical personages introduced are the Earl of Morton and
the Earl of Murray, the bastard brother of the Queen. The attempted delineation of Euphuism in Sir Piercie Shafton and the unfortunate introduction
of the supernatural machinery of the White Lady of Avenel injured the book,
and it was probably the least successful of all Scott's novels. Instead of
being accounted a well-drawn and humourous character of the period, Sir
Piercie was condemned as unnatural and absurd. Sir Walter consoled himself, however, that "the booksellers did not complain of the result of the
" sale of ' The Monastery.' "

A prototype of Captain Clutterbuck, the imaginary editor of " The Monas-
" tery," having been discovered by Robert Chambers in his " Illustrations of
" the Author of Waverley," Sir Walter Scott wrote " that the imaginary editor
" had no real prototype in the village of Melrose or its neighbourhood that
" ever he saw or heard of," and that the identification of Clutterbuck " with
" the neighbour or friend so erroneously identified could never have been
" achieved by any one who had read the book and seen the party alluded to."

MONTEATH, ROBERT: THE FORESTER'S GUIDE AND PROFITABLE
PLANTER. (1827) . . . . . . Pr. xxi. 1

This article appeared in the *Quarterly* for October, 1827, and the reviewer
designates Monteath's work " a useful and interesting treatise." The author
writes " after sixteen years' undeviating attention to the raising young planta-
" tions of considerable extent upon lands which may be, in general, termed
" waste or unimproved," and gives his views in great detail on those points,
in " which the expense of planting is chiefly concerned."

MORIER, JAMES (1780–1849): HAJJI BABA OF ISPAHAN IN ENGLAND.
(1829) . . . . Pr. xviii. 354

This paper appeared in the *Quarterly Review* for January, 1829. The
novel gives the experiences of a Persian in England, and had a wide popularity. Morier, while secretary to the English embassy in Persia, became
versed in the Oriental tongues and customs and, as Scott expressed it, wrote,
thought, and spoke much more like an Oriental than an Englishman.

MY AUNT MARGARET'S MIRROR. (1828) . Nov. xli. 289-346

This was the first of three sketches published in the first volume of "The "Keepsake" for 1828. It is "a mere transcript" of a story the author remembered being struck with in his childhood, as related by a relative who was killed in a fit of insanity by a female attendant who had been attached to her person for half a lifetime. The period of the story is about 1700, in the reign of William III. The infidelity of a husband is disclosed, and the culprit brought to punishment by means of the Magic Mirror.

NACHTSTÜCKE. BY HOFFMANN, ERNEST THEODORE WILLIAM. (1827)

Pr. xviii. 270

See Hoffmann.

NAPOLEON BUONAPARTE, LIFE OF. 9 vols. (1827) . Pr. viii.-xvi.

This is a remarkable monument of good fortune resulting from extraordinary industry. It was published in two years after Scott commenced to collect a wagon-load of folios and quartos to aid in the compilation of this work, receiving such piles of volumes as made his library look like an auctioneer's sales-room. Lockhart records (vol. ix. p. 117) that (allowing for some journeys abroad to collect facts) "the historical task occupied hardly "more than twelve months,—done in the midst of pain, sorrow, and ruin." The first two editions produced for Scott's creditors the enormous sum of £18,000. It was written too hastily to be free from inaccuracies as to minor facts of detail, "but no inaccuracy in the smallest degree affecting the "character of the book as a fair record of great events" was detected even by the critics who severely reviewed it, and among whom were Niebuhr and Lord Macaulay. Samuel Rogers, in his "Recollections," states that the Duke of Wellington, as a military critic, declared it was of "no value." It would have been little short of marvellous had a truly great novelist, a great poet, and an admirable antiquarian student proved himself a "great" historian.

The work opens with a "preliminary view of the French Revolution."

At the end of Pr. vol. x., at pp. 426-427, is given a list of the three hundred and twenty volumes which formed Napoleon's camp library. They were selected by the Emperor, and he wrote out the list in his own hand. The volumes were in 18mo.

It will be observed that "by an original error of the press, which proceeded "too far before it was discovered," the name was "printed with a u—Buona- "parte instead of Bonaparte." Although Sir Walter apologized for this on the ground that Napoleon "always used the last," it seems that the u was used by him in his signature to the contract of marriage between himself and Josephine March 9, 1796, and the omission of the u appears only in documents subsequent to his appointment to the command of the army of Italy.

NEW MAN OF FEELING: FLEETWOOD; OR, THE. BY GODWIN, WILLIAM. (1805) . . . . . . Pr. xviii. 118

See Godwin.

[NORTHANGER ABBEY. BY AUSTEN, JANE. (1821). Pr. xviii. 209

See Austen. The review was written by Archbishop Whately and not by Sir W. Scott.]

OCCASIONAL PIECES NOT CONTAINED IN ANY FORMER EDITION OF SIR WALTER SCOTT'S POETICAL WORKS . . Po. x. 353–380

The selection consists of the eight pieces enumerated below:

Page

BOLD DRAGOON, THE; OR, THE PLAINS OF BADAJOS . . 357

A song written shortly after the Battle of Badajos (April, 1812) for a Yeomanry Cavalry dinner. It is included in George Thomson's " Collection of Select " Melodies," vol. vi.

CARLE, NOW THE KING'S COME 369

These are " new words to an auld spring," and were published as a broadside. They are an imitation of an old Jacobite ditty written on the appearance in the Frith of Forth of the fleet which conveyed King George IV. to Scotland, in August, 1822.

FOR A' THAT AND A' THAT 360

This is entitled " a new song to an old tune." It was sung at the first meeting of the Pitt Club, of Scotland, and is printed in the *Scot's Magazine* for July, 1814.

LINES ADDRESSED TO MONSIEUR ALEXANDRE, THE CELE-BRATED VENTRILOQUIST 363

These are an " Epigram," presented to the ventriloquist in 1824 after an exhibition of his " unrivalled " imitations" at Abbotsford. They are printed in the *Edinburgh Annual Register* of 1824.

LINES ADDRESSED TO RANALD MACDONALD, ESQ., OF STAFFA 356

These are fourteen lines written in the month of August, 1814, in an album kept at the Sound of Ulva Inn.

LINES WRITTEN FOR MISS SMITH 367

These first appeared in the " Forget-Me-Not" for 1834. Miss Smith (the actress) became Mrs. Bartley. The lines were recited at her benefit at the Edinburgh Theatre, in 1817.

OLD MORTALITY. 2 vols. (1816) Nov. ix., 219–374; x. *and* xi. 1–138.

 This was the companion novel to "The Black Dwarf" in the First Series of the "Tales of My Landlord." "Robert Paterson" (1715-1801) "was a real "personage, and received the name of 'Old Mortality' from having devoted his "life to the renovation of the gravestones of the martyrs of the Covenant." He was born in 1715, and gradually became crazed with Cameronianism, neglected the commonest prudential duty of providing for his offspring, and wandered about cleaning moss from gravestones and keeping the letters and effigies on them in good condition. His wife and children were wholly unable to disengage him from this course of living, and he continued it till his death in 1801, in the eighty-sixth year of his age. One of his sons came to America in 1776 and settled at Baltimore. In 1869 Messrs. A. & C. Black caused a headstone of freestone to be erected in Carlaverock Churchyard to the old man's memory. Among the characters in the tale should be studied John Burley (or John Balfour, of Kinloch), the leader of the insurgent Covenanters and murderer of Archbishop Sharp, who "gave a scriptural justification for "all his crimes." His death, as told in "Old Mortality," is fictitious. He really escaped to Holland.

 Peter Poundtext well illustrates the class of preachers whose services caused a considerable schism among the Presbyterians. He was, moreover, an aged pastor, for whom warfare had few charms, "in comparison with a theological "treatise, a pipe, and a jug of ale, which he called his studies." Among the historical characters of this work are the Duke of Monmouth, the natural son of Charles II., and James Grahame, of Claverhouse, whose character, Scott maintained, had been foully traduced, for "he, who was every inch a soldier "and a gentleman, passed among the Scottish vulgar for a ruffian desperado, "who rode a goblin horse, was proof against shot, and in league with the "Devil." This novel was translated into Italian under the title of "The "Scottish Puritans." The period of the story is about 1679-90, in the reigns of Charles II., James II., and of William and Mary.

OMEN, THE. BY GALT, JOHN. (1824) . . . Pr. xviii. 333

    See Galt.

PAUL'S LETTERS TO HIS KINSFOLK. (1816) . . . Pr. v. 1

These were mostly written during Sir W. Scott's tour on the Continent in 1815, directly after the battle of Waterloo. They are, in fact, "a genuine frag-"ment of the author's autobiography." The letters are addressed to four imaginary persons who have, however, been easily identified. The spinster, Sister Margaret, is "only a slender disguise for the author's Aunt Christian "Rutherfurd." The veteran officer, the Major on half pay, is his elder brother, John Scott. The Laird —— ——, Esq., of ——, is Lord Somerville, long president of the Board of Agriculture, and the minister of the gospel at —— is Doctor Douglas, of Galashiels. Many of the letters were printed from the identical sheets that reached Melrose through the post. Letter viii. (pp. 99–145) describes the battle of Waterloo in detail.

Three editions of 6000, 1500, and 1500 copies were disposed of in the course of two or three years.

PEPYS, SAMUEL (1632–1703), MEMOIRS OF. BY BRAYBROOKE, RICH-
    ARD, LORD. (1826) . . . . . Pr. xx. 94

This review appeared in the *Quarterly* for January, 1826. The Diary was written in cipher and lay for one hundred and fifty years in the Pepysian Library bequeathed by the diarist to Magdalen College, Cambridge, England, before the stenographic characters were deciphered. The Diary comprises the first ten years of Mr. Pepys's official life, extending from January, 1659–60, to May, 1669. The revelation of gossip, scandal, anecdote, art, and life as it really was in the time of Charles II. was a real "discovery," and the popularity of this, the first or second best of all "Diaries," will probably stand undiminished for centuries.

At page 149, Sir W. Scott gives a capital outline of the literary "find" of anecdotes, jests, notices of old songs and ballads, and anecdotes of Lely, Faithorne, Holbein, Oliver Cromwell, and Tom Killigrew, with which the "Memoirs" abound.

The description of "a run upon Lombard Street in the days of Charles II.," quoted at page 150, seemed to strike the reviewer with much amusement.

[PERSUASION. BY AUSTEN, JANE. (1821) . . Pr. xviii. 209

    See Austen. The review was written by Archbishop Whately, and not by Sir W. Scott.]

PEVERIL OF THE PEAK. 3 vols. (1823) Nov. xxviii., xxix., *and* xxx.

The novel relates to the period of the pretended Popish Plot, about 1660, in the reign of Charles II. In it we are introduced to Colonel Blood, the

SIR WALTER SCOTT'S WRITINGS

second Duke of Buckingham, Charles II. and Catherine his Consort, Tom Chiffinch, the well-known minister to Charles's pleasures; the Countess of Derby, who defended Lathom House against the Roundheads and was Queen of the Isle of Man; Edward Christian, whose brother had been executed by the Countess of Derby for a political offence; Sir Geoffrey Hudson, the dwarf; Dr. Oates, the discoverer of the pretended Popish Plot, the Duke of Ormond, and Lord Chief Justice Scroggs. These historical characters, with the pretended deaf and dumb attendant, Fenella, and a host of other characters, rather overcrowded the author's canvas. The peculiar laws and state of the Isle of Man are well brought out.

The character of Fenella (or Zarah), the daughter of Edward Christian ("a mere creature of the imagination"), a pretended deaf and dumb fairy-like attendant on the Countess of Derby, was suggested by that of Mignon, the Italian girl, in Goethe's "Wilhelm Meister's Apprenticeship."

PIRATE, THE. 2 vols. (1821) . . . Nov. xxiv. *and* xxv.

The scene of this romance is placed in the Orkney Islands, about the year 1700, in the time of William III. or Queen Anne. The tale is founded on the story of a pirate, named John Gow or Goffe or Smith, who frequented Stromness in 1724-25, and obtained the troth-plight of a young lady of some property only a short time before he was unmasked and, after torture, executed for his many crimes. The wild scenery of the Shetlands is well described.

Interesting peeps are given through the old "Udaller," Magnus Troil, and his fair daughters, Minna and Brenda, into the primitive customs of a remarkable place. A "Udaller" is one who holds lands allodially—that is, free from rent or service-tenure,—in other words, he is a freeholder.

PITCAIRN, ROBERT (1793-1855): CRIMINAL TRIALS IN SCOTLAND FROM 1484 TO 1684. (1831) . . . . Pr. xxi. 199

This article appeared in the *Quarterly* for February, 1831. The work, in ten parts, bound in four quarto volumes, was published under the auspices of the Bannatyne Club, at Edinburgh, of which Sir W. Scott was the founder and first president. This is "the last piece of criticism that came from the "pen of Sir W. Scott." The opening of this interesting review (pp. 199-225) gives a delightful account of the rise of book clubs and the doings of such giants among book collectors as the Duke of Roxburghe and the Earl of Spencer. He relates in detail the history of the sale of "Paradise Lost" for £5 and the subsequent sale of all rights by the bookseller, who was at that time £20 out of pocket, for £25, with many stories of great interest to bibliophiles relating to books, and the Roxburghe, Maitland, and Bannatyne Clubs.

PLANTER'S GUIDE, THE. BY STEUART, SIR HENRY. (1828) Pr. xxi. 77.

See Steuart.

53

PLANTING WASTE LANDS. (1827) . . . . Pr. xxi. 1
  See Monteath.

POETICAL FRAGMENTS . . . . . . Po. vi. 373–382
  See Fragments.

POETS, SPECIMENS OF THE EARLY ENGLISH. BY ELLIS, GEORGE.
  (1804) . . . . Pr. xvii. 1
  See Ellis.

[PONTEFRACT CASTLE. BY THE AUTHOR OF WAVERLEY.

> This was a forgery (*see* "Count Robert of Paris"), and is here mentioned simply as a fact of interest in connection with Sir W. Scott's literary career.]

POPULAR POETRY, ESSAY ON. (1830) . . . Po. i. 5–91

> This is an introduction to "Minstrelsy of the Scottish Border," and "in a "cursory manner" goes through the history of English and Scottish poetry. It notices the principal collections which had from time to time been formed of such compositions. "These remarks were first appended to the edition "of 1830." It has eight appendixes.

PROSE WORKS, THE . . . . lxi.–xc.

PROVINCIAL ANTIQUITIES OF SCOTLAND. (1818) . Pr. vii. 155

> These are a series of "topographical and historical essays which originally "appeared in the successive numbers of the splendidly illustrated work called "'Provincial Antiquities of Scotland.'" Scott refused to accept payment for these articles, but when the success of the work was assured, "accepted "from the proprietors some of the beautiful drawings by J. M. W. Turner, "Rev. J. Thomson Callcott, Nasmyth, and other artists which had been pre- "pared to accompany his text." The drawings were placed in the little breakfast room at Abbotsford. The subjects of these essays are:

	Page
BASS ROCK, THE	438
BORTHWICK CASTLE	196
BORTHWICK CASTLE (THE GREAT HALL) . . .	214
CRAIGMILLAR CASTLE	363
CRICHTON CASTLE	157
DALKEITH, TOWN OF	216
DIRLETON CASTLE	405
DUNBAR, CASTLE OF	410
EDINBURGH, ENTRANCE TO LEITH HARBOR . .	280
EDINBURGH, FROM BRAID HILLS . . .	247
EDINBURGH, FROM CORSTORPHINE HILL . . .	275

QUEEN-HOO HALL. (1807–1808) . . . Nov. i., lxv.–xc.

Sir W. Scott undertook for Messrs. Murray to arrange for publication some posthumous productions of Mr. John Strutt, of "Horda Angel Cynnan" fame, and finding among that author's papers an unfinished romance entitled "Queen-hoo Hall," Scott undertook to supply "such a hasty" conclusion "as could be shaped out from the story of which Mr. Strutt had laid the "foundation." Chapters iv. and v. by the author of "Waverley" are here given. "Queen-hoo Hall" "was not very successful."

QUENTIN DURWARD. 2 vols. (1823) . . Nov. xxxi. and xxxii.

The story is laid at Plessis les Tours, and relates to Louis XI. of France and Charles the Bold, Duke of Burgundy, about the year 1470, in the time of Edward IV. of England.

When first published it created as great a sensation in France as "Waver-"ley" had done on its first appearance in England. It is one of Scott's most interesting tales, and the general appreciation has been much enhanced by the stage versions of the character of Louis XI., which proved so masterly in the hands of Charles Kean and his successor in the character, Sir Henry Irving.

Among the historical personages introduced are John, Cardinal Balue; Charles the Bold; Lord Crawford, the captain of the Archers of the Scottish Guard; De la Marck, the Wild Boar of Ardennes; Philip de Comines; Princess Joan; Prince Louis of Bourbon; the Bishop of Liége; the Dauphin, afterwards Louis XII., whose miserable chamber in Plessis is still shown; Galeotti, the astrologer; and Louis XI. himself, with his strange surroundings, Oliver, the barber, and Tristan l'Hermite, the hangman.

Some of the oubliettes so graphically described by Sir W. Scott, and the cage in which the Cardinal de la Balue was confined for eleven years for betraying the king's secrets to the Duke of Burgundy, are still to be seen by the visitors to the old castle of Plessis les Tours.

RADCLIFFE, MRS. ANN (1764–1823), MEMOIR OF. (1821–5) Pr. iii. 337.

This is one of the " Prefaces" in Ballantyne's " Novelist's Library." Few persons read Mrs. Radcliffe's novels now, and according to W. H. Prescott she was "good for nothing out of the region of the picturesque, except when in " her horrors." Having gained a name by her " Romance of the Forest," she was paid £500 for her " Mysteries of Udolpho," and £800 for " The " Italian; or, The Confessional of the Black Penitent : A Romance."

Leigh Hunt, in his " Men, Women, and Books," says that the authoress's poems are unworthy of her romances. In the latter she was "the mighty " magician of Udolpho;" in her verses she is "a tinselled nymph in a panto- " mime, calling up commonplaces with a wand."

Mr. Edward Cheney, in conversation with Sir W. Scott, maintained (see Lockhart's " Life," vol. x. p. 193) that "the Utopian scenes and manner " of Mrs. Radcliffe's novels captivated the imagination more than the most " laboured descriptions or the greatest historical accuracy."

REDGAUNTLET. 2 vols. (1824) . . . Nov. xxxv. and xxxvi.

The story relates to a conspiracy formed by Sir Edward Hugh Redgauntlet about 1770, in the time of George III., on behalf of the exiled Charles Edward Stuart, then above forty years of age. The refusal of the prince to dismiss Miss Walkinshaw, his mistress, is made a pivot of the story, which is mainly in the form of letters. Scott at first wanted to call it " Herries," but at last yielded to the persuasions of Constable and Ballantyne, and changed the name to " Redgauntlet."

Lockhart remarks (see " Life," vol. vii. p. 214) that "with posterity, " assuredly this novel will yield in interest to none of the series; for it con- " tains, perhaps, more of the author's personal experiences than any other of " them, or even than all the rest put together."

REEVE, CLARA (1725–1803), MEMOIR OF. (1821–5) . Pr. iii. 325

This is one of the " Prefaces" in Ballantyne's " Novelist's Library." It is difficult to see why Clara Reeve's tales were selected for the " Novelist's " Library," or why, if such authoresses were selected, it should be wondered that no demand existed for copies of the reissue. Her principal work was " The Old English Baron," first published as " The Champion of Virtue : " A Gothic Story." She received £10 for the copyright. It was avowedly written in imitation of Walpole's " Otranto," of which romance the authoress termed her own novel "the literary offspring," but, as Walpole remarked, " it was wholly reduced to reason and probability," and so probable in its incidents "that any trial for murder at the Old Bailey would make a more "interesting story." It is as forgotten as her volume of "Poems," 1769, "published for subscribers," who do not appear to have made a profitable investment.

RELIGIOUS DISCOURSES, TWO. (1828.)

These are two discourses written by Sir Walter for Mr. Huntley Gordon (1796–1868) under peculiar circumstances. They are included in some editions of Scott's writings to complete his prose works, but not in the one now under description. Mr. Gordon was acting as amanuensis for the novelist, but purposing to enter the Scotch ministry. He was much distressed about two trial sermons he had to prepare. The novelist said, "You get on "with your work, and I will prepare your sermons," and two days later he handed to Mr. Gordon the manuscripts of these sermons. In the end Mr. Gordon wrote two for himself, feeling conscientious scruples about preaching those prepared by another, and passed the dreadful ordeal with success. The kindliness of Scott's action was not diminished.

RELIQUES OF BURNS: COLLECTED BY CROMEK, R. H. (1809) Pr. xvii. 242.

See Burns.

RICHARDSON, SAMUEL (1689–1761), MEMOIR OF . . Pr. iii. 3–76

This is one of the "Prefaces" in Ballantyne's "Novelist's Library." Richardson has been called "the founder of the English domestic novel." He was addicted as a boy to letter writing, and his novels were all written in the form of letters. His principal writings were "Pamela; or, Virtue Rewarded," "Clarissa Harlowe; or, The History of a Young Lady," and the "History of "Sir Charles Grandison."

RITSON, JOSEPH (1752–1803): ANCIENT ENGLISH METRICAL RO-MANCES, SELECTED BY JOSEPH RITSON. (1806) Pr. xvii. 16

This is an article published in the *Edinburgh Review* for 1806, contrasting the "Metrical Romances" edited by George Ellis with those edited by "the "ingenious but whimsical and crabbed antiquarian," Mr. Ritson.

RITSON, JOSEPH: ANNALS OF THE CALEDONIANS, PICTS, AND SCOTS, ETC. (1829) . . . . . . Pr. xx. 301

This review appeared in the *Quarterly* for July, 1829. It criticises a posthumous publication of Ritson, of whom and by whom probably harder words were bandied between reviewers and reviewed than by or concerning any other writer in the English language. He lived in a state of bitter and unremitted warfare with beefsteaks and Revelation, his best friends, and half the letters in the alphabet. Much of his pedantry and ill-judged language may be excused on the ground that his mind was diseased. He died insane.

ROB ROY. 2 vols. (1817) . . . . Nov. vii. *and* viii.

This is "Francis Osbaldistone's Autobiography," and the scene is laid at the period of the rebellion of 1715. The first edition of this novel was of ten thousand copies, and yet in three weeks a second impression of three thousand was called for. The title of the book was suggested by Mr. Constable, the publisher, Sir Walter feeling great hesitation as to the best to select. No traveller in Scotland can sail about Loch Lomond without finding spot after spot consecrated to the memory of the scenes and events in which the celebrated clan of MacGregor was concerned. Rob Roy (1660–1743), the adored chieftain of the MacGregors, was a partisan of Prince Charles Edward in the rebellion of 1715, and has been styled the "Robin Hood of Scotland," who could be very crafty, but was kind to the poor and never cruel. The Duke of Montrose having seized Rob Roy's lands, the latter carried on a war of reprisals for many years, and became widely celebrated for his exploits.

A version of this novel was put on the London stage, and its popularity still exists. The novelist was enthusiastic over it, especially the representation of "Bailie Nicol Jarvie," which he thought inimitable. (*See* Lockhart's "Life," vol. vi. p. 62.) It was specially selected by King George IV. for representation in 1822.

ROKEBY. (1812) . . . . Po. ix. 1–353

This, the fourth of Sir W. Scott's principal poems, was characterized by the author as something like new ground, inasmuch as it "turned upon char-"acter, as the force of the 'Lay' was thrown on style, in 'Marmion' on de-"scription, and in the 'Lady of the Lake' on incident." Scott wrote in 1812 that the Matilda of the poem was "attempted for the existing person of a lady "who is now no more," and was the object of his first unfortunate love. It has never been much of a favourite with the general body of readers. Still, only eighty copies remained unsold of the first edition of three thousand two hundred and fifty after the second day of publication. It was just at this time that Lord Byron brought out the first two cantos of his "Childe Harold," and Scott recognized the greatness of his competitor at once. Rokeby is near Greta Bridge, in Yorkshire. The date of the supposed events is immediately subsequent to the great battle of Marston Moor, July 3, 1644.

ROMANCE, ESSAY ON. (1824) . . . . . Pr. v. 127

This is included in the Chronological List of Scott's writings under the year 1823. It was first published in the Supplement of the "Encyclopædia "Britannica" in 1824. The writer was paid £100 for the essay.

Sir W. Scott treats of his subject under three heads: (p. 133) the general history and origin of this peculiar species of composition, and particularly of the romances relating to European chivalry; (p. 189) the history of the romance of chivalry in the different states of Europe; and (p. 213) the various kinds of romantic composition by which the ancient romances of chivalry were followed and superseded.

Rose, William Stewart (1775–1843): Amadis de Gaul, Poetical Version of. (1803) . . . . . Pr. xviii. 40

This was reviewed in Scott's first contribution to the *Edinburgh Review* with Southey's prose version of the same romance from the Spanish. Mr. Rose took his translation from the French of Nicolas de Herberay.

Russell, James: Murder of Archbishop Sharp. (1818) Pr. xix. 273.

See Kirkton *and* Sharp.

Sadler, or Sadleir, Sir Ralph (1507–1587), Memoir of. (1809) Pr. iv. 71

This memoir was originally prefixed to an edition of Sadler's "State "Papers," published at Edinburgh in 1809.

This statesman led an exciting career. He rose largely under the auspices of Thomas Cromwell, and received large grants of lands stolen from the Church by Henry VIII. He went into private life during the reign of Queen Mary, but emerged into political life on the accession of Elizabeth, and was one of her trusted servants for twenty-nine years. He was appointed keeper of Mary, Queen of Scots, on her imprisonment at Tutbury, and it was of Sadler that the complaints were made that he had allowed that unhappy princess to hawk whilst on her road from one prison to another.

Saint Ronan's Well. 2 vols. (1823) . Nov. xxxiii. *and* xxxiv.

This novel was a picture of modern life about the year 1800, in the reign of George III., and the scene was laid at Inverleithen upon Tweed, in Peebleshire, the St. Ronan's Well of the tale. The critics were divided, those south of the Tweed declaring that Sir Walter had outwritten himself "and "committed a literary suicide in this unhappy attempt," but the Scots, and the Inverleithenites in particular, were delighted. The name of Inverleithen was abolished, the quiet of the out-of-the-world nook was lost, and in place of the long neglected Well, there sprang up "spruce bottles and huge staring lodg-"ing-houses, and on the corner of every new erection you may read Ab-"botsford Place, Waverley Row, The Marmion Hotel, or some inscription of "the like coinage."

The character of Meg Dods, the old landlady of the Clachan or Mowbray Arms Inn, is regarded as "one of the very best low comedy characters in the "whole range of fiction."

A portrait of Sir W. Scott with his dog, from the painting of John Watson Gordon, and dated 1830, is given as a frontispiece to Nov. xxxiii.

Saint Valentine's Day. (1828) . . . Nov. xlii. *and* xliii.

See Fair Maid of Perth.

SALMONIA; OR, DAYS OF FLY-FISHING. BY DAVY, SIR HUMPHRY.
(1828) . . . . Pr. xx. 245

This review appeared in the *Quarterly* for October, 1828. "Salmonia"
was written by Sir Humphry Davy, "the greatest chemical genius that ever
"appeared," in the intervals of "many months of severe and dangerous ill-
"ness." One of the great sources of interest in this article will be found in
the "sweet episodes of personal reminiscence" with which it abounds.

SCOTLAND: ANNALS OF THE CALEDONIANS, PICTS, AND SCOTS, ETC.
(1829) . . . . Pr. xx. 301

See Ritson.

SCOTLAND, CRIMINAL TRIALS IN, FROM 1484 TO 1684. BY PITCAIRN,
ROBERT. (1831) . . . . . Pr. xxi. 199

See Pitcairn.

SCOTLAND, HISTORY OF. 5 vols. (1827-29) . . Pr. xxii.-xxvi.

See Tales of a Grandfather.

SCOTLAND, HISTORY OF. BY TYTLER, PATRICK FRASER. Pr. xxi.
152.

See Tytler.

SCOTLAND, HISTORY OF CHURCH OF. BY KIRKTON, REV. JAMES.
(1818) . . . . Pr. xix. 213

See Kirkton.

SCOTLAND, PROVINCIAL ANTIQUITIES OF. (1818) . Pr. vii. 155

See Provincial.

SCOTLAND, SKETCH OF THE HISTORY OF.

This was a contribution to "Lardner's Cyclopædia," and it is understood
that permission to include a copy among Scott's prose works was not given.
It can be found in the "Cyclopædia" in question. It extended only to 1603,
whereas the history in the "Tales of a Grandfather" brought down the story
to the close of the rebellion of 1745.

SCOTT, THOMAS (*ob.* 1823). . . . . Nov. i., xci.-xcvi.

Thomas was third brother of Sir Walter, who gives an interesting account
(Nov. i. xxxiii.-xxxv.) of his attempt to persuade Thomas to become an author.
A subject and a hero were selected, but "he never wrote a single line of the

" projected work." The " Author of Waverley" here gives " a simple anecdote
" on which" the proposed tale of fiction by his brother was to be founded.

As to the suggestion once made that he was the veritable " Author of
" Waverley," *see* Lockhart's " Life," vol. iv. p. 400.

SCOTT, SIR WALTER (1771–1832), MEMOIRS OF. BY LOCKHART, JOHN
GIBSON. 10 vols. (1836) . . . . . L. i.-x.

This " Life" was Mr. Lockhart's most important work, and is " surpassed in
" interest by few, if any, biographies in the English language." He married
Sophia, the eldest daughter of Sir Walter; but his wife and two sons predeceased him, leaving his daughter the only surviving descendant of Sir W.
Scott when she was married to Mr. Hope, who assumed the name of Scott.

At the end of the tenth volume (pp. 269–359) are in an appendix,—

The work executed by Sir W. Scott was enormous. In thirty-five years he
produced ten volumes of poems, twenty-five novels, several short tales, twelve
volumes of " Tales of a Grandfather," besides the " History of Scotland,
" from the time of Macbeth to 1760," the " History of France," the " Lives of
" Novelists," the " Life of Napoleon Buonaparte," in nine volumes, and
reviews and contributions to periodicals; besides editing Dean Swift's works
in nineteen volumes, and Dryden's works in eighteen volumes, each preceded
by a valuable " Life."

The story of Scott's travelling back to Abbotsford to die, and his joy at
being once more in that so dearly-loved home, has often been told. Louise
Moulton, speaking of Abbotsford, says : " The most interesting room is the
" library. It is the largest of all the rooms, measuring fifty feet by sixty. Its
" roof is of richly-carved oak, modelled after Roslin and Melrose. Its books
" number at least twenty thousand volumes, many of them extremely rare and
" valuable. They are placed in carved oaken cases, under lock and key.
" Among the adornments of the room are Chantrey's bust of Scott, a copy of
" the Stratford bust of Shakespeare, a silver urn presented by Lord Byron, an
" ebony writing-desk presented by a royal George, and two beautifully-carved
" arm-chairs presented by the Pope." Abbotsford and Dryburgh, where Scott
is buried, are two sacred spots, visited by thousands every year.

SCOTTISH POETRY, CHRONICLE OF, FROM THE THIRTEENTH CENTURY
TO THE UNION OF THE CROWNS, WITH A GLOSSARY. (1803.)

See Sibbald.

SERAPIONS-BRÜDER. BY HOFFMANN, ERNEST THEODORE WILLIAM.
(1827) . . . . Pr. xviii. 270
See Hoffmann.

SEWARD, MISS ANNA (1747–1809), MEMOIR OF. (1810) Pr. iv. 199

This sketch was originally prefixed to Scott's edition of Miss Seward's
"Poetical Works," published in 1810. This reissue was executed by Sir W.
Scott at the request of the authoress shortly before her death. The choice of
this lady's effusions was among the most unfortunate that James Ballantyne
selected, and his brother "printed in deference to the wishes of the editor."
At the same time, Sir W. Scott's truer judgment enabled him to write to Miss
Joanna Baillie, "I am now doing penance . . . by submitting to edit her
"posthumous poetry, most of which is absolutely execrable." Horace Walpole wrote of the efforts of this versifier that the "Misses Seward and Williams,
"and half a dozen more of such harmonious virgins, have no imagination, no
"novelty. Their thoughts and phrases are like their gowns,—old remnants
"cut and turned."

SHARP, JAMES, ARCHBISHOP (1618–1679), MURDER OF. BY RUSSELL,
JAMES, AN ACTOR THEREIN. (1818) . . Pr. xix. 273

This review appeared in the *Quarterly* for January, 1818. It reveals a
strange state of "religious" feeling in Scotland at that distracted period.

See Kirkton.

SHELLEY, MARY (1797–1851): FRANKENSTEIN ; OR, THE MODERN
PROMETHEUS (1818) . . . . . Pr. xviii. 250

See Frankenstein.

SIBBALD, J. : CHRONICLE OF SCOTTISH POETRY FROM THE THIRTEENTH
CENTURY TO THE UNION OF THE CROWNS, WITH A GLOSSARY.
(1803.)

This is a review which appeared in the *Edinburgh Review* for October,
1803, in the same number with Sir Walter's first contribution on Southey's
"Amadis of Gaul." It has not been included in this edition of Scott's prose
works. Scott regards the "Glossary" as "a very important national acqui-
"sition." Sir Walter's remarks on the make up of the book are interesting at
this distance of ninety-four years from when the complaint of bad workman-
ship was contrasted with over-splendour. He says :
"We are no great admirers of fashionable printing, hot-press work, or
"cream-colored paper, yet we could have wished that this useful book had
"been executed in something of a better style. We do not say that it is inac-
"curately printed ; and certainly, as was recommended by Lord Chesterfield
"to George Faulknor, the paper *is* somewhat *whitish*, and the ink rather *black-*

"*ish;* but a Chronicle of National Poetry should not be printed quite like
"the 'Cheap Repository,' or the 'Pilgrim's Progress.' The paper is of so in-
"ferior a quality as not to stand the press; so that most copies we have seen
"are much damaged and torn; besides which, the printer's or bookseller's
"devils, entertaining probably little respect for the external appearance of Mr.
"Sibbald's labours, have folded the sheets with cruel inaccuracy. These are
"evils which require to be checked where they occur, as much as the opposite
"extreme of absurd and expensive decoration."

SMITH, CHARLOTTE (1749–1806), MEMOIR OF. (1821–25) Pr. iv. 20

This was written to appear as one of the " Prefaces" in Ballantyne's " Nov-
"elist's Library," but the publication of that series had ceased before the
" Memoir" saw light. Charlotte Smith made an imprudent marriage before
she was sixteen, and underwent a life-long punishment from pecuniary and
domestic troubles, which involved herself and her twelve children in endless
troubles and misfortunes. She was an industrious authoress, and translated
Prévost's " Manon Lescaut," besides writing some twenty-two works of her
own. Sir W. Scott has published this " Memoir," which was written by
Mrs. Dorset (Mrs. Smith's sister), adding some critical notices of his own, in
which his kindness of heart prevailed to an unusual extent even for him.
He praised highly where little praise can be properly bestowed. Sir Archibald Alison pronounces Mrs. Smith's novels as " well-nigh unreadable," and
Prof. George Moir criticises her fictions as " extremely defective in plot, and
"marked with signs of haste."

SMOLLETT, TOBIAS GEORGE (1721–1771), MEMOIR OF. (1821–25)
Pr. iii. 117

This is one of the " Prefaces" in Ballantyne's " Novelist's Library." Smollett is generally believed to have painted a few " of his own early adventures
"under the veil of fiction," and some of his principal characters have been
identified with probable prototypes. For example, Narcissa, in " Roderick
" Random," was supposed to be Mrs. Smollett, the author himself, Roderick,
and a book-binder named Lewis, of Chelsea, was depicted in Strap. Two
naval officers under whom Smollett served were stigmatized as Oakum and
Whaffle. So, in later years, he described many of his own peculiarities
under the character of Matthew Bramble in " Humphrey Clinker."

Towards the end of his life Sir W. Scott commented a good deal on the
singularity that Fielding and Smollett " had both been driven abroad by de-
"clining health, and never returned," doubtless applying it to his then con-
templated voyage abroad in the vain search for restored health.

The unsavory tale, entitled " Memoirs of a Lady of Quality," interpolated
in " Peregrine Pickle" contains the history of Lady Vane, equally celebrated
for her beauty and her intrigues. Smollett, unhappily for his own reputation,
accepted a handsome fee for inserting her story. He contributed the Histories of France, Italy, and Germany to the " Modern Universal History."

SOMERVILLE, JOHN, LORD (1819), CHARACTER OF THE LATE. (1819)
Pr. iv. 309

This was published in the *Edinburgh Weekly Journal* of October 27, 1819.
Lord Somerville's "favourite studies were of an agricultural nature, and
"respected the growth of stock, the improvement of land, and the other
"objects of national economy." He succeeded to the title in 1796 on the
death of his uncle. Scott said of him, "a warmer heart was never made cold
"by death."

SONGS . . . . . . Po. vi. 361–382

The four songs included are:

		Page
DYING BARD, THE	. . . .	. . 366
HELVELLYN	. . . . .	. . 370
MAID OF TORO, THE	. . .	. . 368
NORMAN HORSESHOE, THE	. .	. . 363

SONGS AND MISCELLANIES . . . . . Po. xi. 293–382

This selection consists of twenty-eight pieces enumerated below, several of
which are worthy of notice for themselves, and others on account of the events
they commemorate.

Page
BANNATYNE CLUB, THE (1823) 377
  Written for the anniversary dinner of March, 1823.
  Sir W. Scott was first president of the club, which was
  instituted in 1822 for the publication or reprint of rare
  and curious works connected with the history and antiquities of Scotland.

DANCE OF DEATH, THE (1815) 297
  This was first published in the *Edinburgh Annual
  Register*, vol. v. Written in view of the terrible slaugh-
  ter at Waterloo.

DONALD CAIRD'S COME AGAIN (1818) 328
  Donald the Tinker, or Caird, was written for "Al-
  "byn's Anthology."

DUNOIS, ROMANCE OF (1815) 304
  This is from the French, and appeared in 1815 in
  "Paul's Letters" (Pr. v. 159) and in the *Edinburgh
  Annual Register*. Attributed "to a manuscript collec-
  "tion of French songs," which was found on the field
  of Waterloo, and had probably been compiled by some
  young officer.

SOUTHEY, ROBERT (1774-1843): AMADIS DE GAUL, PROSE VERSION OF.
(1803) . . . . Pr. xviii. 1

This was Scott's first contribution to the *Edinburgh Review*, and was included in the number for October, 1803. After years of forgetfulness, into
which this romance had fallen, except as one of the three spared by the
Curate in " Don Quixote," it was strange that Southey and William Stewart
Rose should both at one time give to the world a prose and a poetical version
of this romance, which is, as the Curate expressed it, " the first of its kind
" and the best."

The earliest known edition of this romance by Vasco de Lobeira (1360?–
1403) was printed in 1519. The celebrated translation by Nicolas de Herberay was published in 1540. Of this romance Saintsbury says that " to no
" single book can be so clearly traced the heroic romances of the early seven-
" teenth century."

SOUTHEY, ROBERT: BUNYAN, JOHN, LIFE OF. (1830) Pr. xviii. 74

This appeared in the *Quarterly Review* for 1830. The charge that Bunyan
did not write the " Pilgrim's Progress" is as old as the days of the author himself, who has been described somewhat oddly by Isaac Disraeli as the " Spen-
" ser of the people." In " what Bunyan considered verses," prefixed to the
" Holy War," he writes :

" Some say the ' Pilgrim's Progress' is not mine,
" Insinuating as if I would shine
" In a name and fame by the worth of another,
" Like some made rich by robbing of their brother;
*   *   *   *   *   *   *
" It came from mine heart, so to my head,
" And thence into my fingers trickled;
" Then to my pen, from whence, immediately
" On paper did I dribble it daintily."

The theory that the tinker of Elstow whilst in Bedford prison amused himself by translating this immortal book from a " Latin manuscript" is amusing, and answers itself by being simply stated.

SOUTHEY, ROBERT: CHRONICLE OF THE CID. (1809) Pr. xviii.   44

This appeared in the *Quarterly Review* for February, 1809.

The Cid (1040–1099) is the principal national hero of Spain, famous for his exploits in the wars with the Moors. Professor Dozy (the Orientalist) has written a work to prove that the Cid was a cruel monster, and his generally accepted history " a tissue of inventions." Poole says in his " Story of the " Moors" that " the best popular account of the hero (Rodrigo Diaz de Bivar) " in discriminating hands and with due allowances is still Southey's fascinating " ' Chronicle.' "

After lavish praise the reviewer complains of " sundry odd phrases which " we could have wished amended," but abstains from dwelling on the point " because Mr. Southey has informed us (page 73) that reviewers, in censuring " his introduction of new words, have only shown their own ignorance of the " English language."

SOUTHEY, ROBERT: CURSE OF KEHAMA (1811).   . Pr. xvii.   301

This article appeared in the *Quarterly Review* for February, 1811. Of this review Scott wrote to Ellis: " I have run up an attempt on the ' Curse of " ' Kehama' for the *Quarterly;* a strange thing it is,—the ' Curse,' I mean,— " and the critic is not, as the blackguards say, worth a damn; but what I " could I did, which was to throw as much weight as possible upon the beau- " tiful passages, of which there are many, and to slur over the absurdities, of " which there are not a few." (*See* Lockhart's " Life," vol. iii. p. 262.) The faults of Southey's poem " lie on the surface, . . . but its beauties are infinite, " and it possesses that high qualification for popularity,—the power of exciting " a painful and sustained interest."

SPENSER, EDMUND (1553–1598), WORKS OF. BY TODD (REV.), JOHN. (1805)   .   .   .   . Pr. xvii.   80

See Todd.

Sporting Tour, A, through the Northern Parts of England and Great Part of the Highlands of Scotland. By Thornton, Colonel Thomas. (1805) . Pr. xix. 87

See Thornton.

Sterne, Laurence (1713-1768), Memoir of. (1821-25) Pr. iii. 273.

This is one of the " Prefaces" in Ballantyne's " Novelist's Library." It is largely composed of the autobiographical memorandum left by Sterne. Sterne was a terrible plagiarist, and in his " Tristram Shandy" laid many great authors under contribution. He is styled by Dr. Ferriar " a ruthless plun- "derer of other men's goods." Horace Walpole thought him tiresome; Goldsmith styled him " a dull fellow;" Hazlitt declared that " his works only "consist of morceaux,—of brilliant passages;" and Thackeray wrote that "he was a great jester, not a great humourist." But plagiarist or not, his "Tristram Shandy" and "Sentimental Journey" will hold their place in literature for centuries.

Sterne has personified himself in many ways in the " Parson Yorick," but, as Scott remarks, "there are shades of simplicity thrown into the character of ' Yorick' which did not exist in that of Sterne." Dr. Slop has been iden- tified with Dr. Burton, of York, who published a treatise on midwifery in 1751.

Steuart, Sir Henry (*ob.* 1836): Planter's Guide, The; or, A Practical Essay on the Best Method of giving Immedi- ate Effect to Wood, by the removal of Large Trees and Underwood. (1828) . . . . Pr. xxi. 77

This article appeared in the *Quarterly* for March, 1828. In Scott's diary is entered the remark, " Sir Henry Steuart is lifted beyond the solid earth by "the effect of his book's success; but the book well deserves it." This was upon transplanting a tree, "which was performed with great ease."

Suffolk, Henrietta, Countess of, Correspondence of: Croker, Right Hon. John Wilson. (1824) . . Pr. xix. 185

See Croker.

Surgeon's Daughter, The. (1827) . . Nov. xlviii. 147-430

This was the third tale of the First Series of the " Chronicles of the Canon- "gate," but afterwards styled "part of the Second Series" of those Chroni- cles. The story relates to the period of 1750-70, in the reigns of George II. and George III. The story of the principal incident was narrated to Sir Walter by his friend, Mr. Train. The villany of the pretended lover who for bribes could decoy an innocent maiden to India to be a concubine in the harem of Tippoo Saib is founded on fact. The crime was fortunately prevented at the last moment, and the perfidious lover was killed in the affray that arose on the rescue of the betrayed maiden.

SWIFT, JONATHAN, D.D. (1667–1745), MEMOIRS OF. (1814) Pr. ii.

This was published in "The Works of Jonathan Swift, with Notes and "a Life," in nineteen volumes. For this undertaking Constable paid Scott the munificent sum of £1500. The object of Sir W. Scott in this Life seemed to be to recognize and dwell upon the superb and enormous talents of his author, and to overlook, or at least deal gently with, the foibles and worse traits of the dean's character, which arose, to what extent can never be ascertained, from the inscrutable and unexplained disease that marred his life from the time when he celebrated his early birthdays by reading, on each recurring festival, the lamentation of Job, as to the day when it was said in his house that a man-child was born, to the end when his life was quenched in helpless idiocy. Lord Jeffrey, in his review of this Life, complained that the bad side of the dean's life was too sparingly dealt with. Would that the majority of biographers were willing to write with the lenient thoughts of Sir W. Scott. The volume has a frontispiece and title, a portrait of the dean, and a view of Swift's monument in St. Patrick's Cathedral, Dublin.

TALES OF A GRANDFATHER: FRANCE, HISTORY OF. 2 vols. (1830)
Pr. xxvii.–xxviii.

These tales were, like the Scottish Stories, addressed to John Hugh Lockhart, Sir Walter's grandson. The history of France is only brought down to 1414, when Henry V. of England had just succeeded to the English throne, and who "breathed nothing at his accession save invasion against his "neighbours," and who fought the memorable battle of Agincourt in the following year, 1415.

TALES OF A GRANDFATHER: SCOTLAND, HISTORY OF. 5 vols. (1827–
29) . . . . Pr. xxii.–xxvi.

Characteristically of Sir W. Scott, the day he finished the "Life of Napo-"leon" he conceived the idea of writing these stories on the history of Scotland "somewhat in the manner of Croker's on that of England." They were written for his invalid grandson, affectionately nicknamed Hugh Littlejohn, Esquire. The lad was at that time so far restored to health that he was able to sit on his pony again, and the great author rode daily among the woods with his Hugh Littlejohn (the son of Mr. and Mrs. Lockhart) and told the tale, thus ascertaining that it suited the comprehension of boyhood before he reduced it to writing. Sir Walter took great delight in the wild times in which, at least, there could be "no fear of want of interest, no lassitude," in the days described,—

" For treason, d'ye see,
" Was to them a dish of tea,
" And murder, bread and butter."

The reception of these tales by the public " was more rapturous than that " of any one of his works since ' Ivanhoe.' " These tales were published in three series of three volumes each,—the first series in 1827, the second in 1828, and the third in 1829. The period covered in them ranges from Macbeth to 1760, " when the two sister nations had become blended together in " manners as well as political ties."

John Hugh Lockhart, to whom these tales were addressed, predeceased his grandfather on the 15th of December, 1831, in the eleventh year of his age.

TALES OF MY LANDLORD. Third Edition. (1817) . Pr. xix. 1

This review appeared in the *Quarterly* for January, 1817. It was " prompted " by the appearance of a series of essays in a religious magazine (*The Chris-* " *tian Instructor*)," in which Dr. Thomas McCrie " bitterly impugned the " views given of the Scotch Covenanters in the ' Waverley Novels.' " The materials of this article were in part collected by William Erskine, Lord Kinnedder, but the manuscript, " now in the possession of Mr. Murray, is entirely in " the handwriting of Sir Walter himself." It is believed that Erskine wrote " the critical estimate of the ' Waverley Novels' which it embraces, although " for the purpose of mystification Scott had taken the trouble to transcribe the " paragraphs in which that estimate is contained." (Lockhart's " Life," vol. v. p. 174.) The article is doubly interesting, as showing the clever way in which the author could write in pursuance of his determined love for anonymity. It refers to the transatlantic report circulated at that time that the " Waverley Novels" were acknowledged by Sir Walter's brother Thomas to have been written by the latter. The last paragraph is described by Lockhart as one " over which a misanthrope might have chuckled."

" In this article," Scott says, are contained " illustrations of the novels" with which he supplied his accomplished friend, who took the trouble to write the review.

In it will be found the original of Meg Merrilies and one or two other personages of the same cast of character.

TALISMAN, THE. (1825) . . . . . . Nov. xxxviii.

This and " The Betrothed" constitute " The Tales of the Crusaders." The romance is laid in the time of Richard I., about the year 1193, during the truce with Saladin which preceded the abandonment of the crusade that had been led by Richard. " The Talisman" was a pebble possessing medicinal properties, and belonged to Saladin. He kept it in a silken purse. It was dipped into a goblet of water, that was then given to a patient to drink and be cured.

Among the historical characters introduced are Queen Berengaria, King Richard's consort; Philip Augustus of France; Richard Cœur de Lion; Saladin; and the Earl of Salisbury, King Richard's bastard brother; Conrade of Montserrat; and Sir Thomas Multon, the faithful follower of King Richard.

TAPESTRIED CHAMBER, THE; OR, THE LADY IN THE SACQUE. (1828)
Nov. xli. 347-373

This was the second of three sketches published in "The Keepsake" for 1828. Sir W. Scott heard the story from Miss Anna Seward. It is a story of the year 1780, in the reign of George III.

TASCHEREAU, JULES ANTOINE (1801-1874): HISTOIRE DE LA VIE ET
DES ŒUVRES DE MOLIÈRE . . . Pr. xvii. 137
See Molière.

THEATRICAL FUND DINNER . . . Nov. xli., xxxv.-lxxiii.

This gives an account of the dinner at Edinburgh at which the anonymity of Sir W. Scott was finally abandoned, and at which he stated in emerging *nominis umbrâ* that "he was the 'Author of Waverley,'" and that "when "he said he was the author, he was the total and undivided author, for, with "the exception of quotations, there was not a single word that was not de- "rived from himself or suggested in the course of his reading."

THOMAS THE RHYMER . . . . . . Nov. i., xli.-liv.

This is a fragment of a romance which was to have been thus entitled. It was "the first attempt at romantic composition by an author who has"—he is writing thirty years later—"since written so much in that department." Scott abandoned the idea, as the "legend would have formed but an unhappy "foundation for a prose story, and must have degenerated into a mere fairy "tale." (*See* Po. iv. 110-166, *and* Tristrem.)

THORNTON, COLONEL THOMAS (*ob.* 1823): A SPORTING TOUR
THROUGH THE NORTHERN PARTS OF ENGLAND AND GREAT
PART OF THE HIGHLANDS OF SCOTLAND. (1805) Pr. xix. 87

This review appeared in the *Edinburgh* for January, 1805. It is full of humour, and makes great fun over the fact that through this tour "scarcely "a Gaelic name is properly spelled." The nature of Thornton's tour did not strike the reviewer as deserving elaborate description, but he pleads that if the good colonel desired to tell the details it would only be justifiable if told over a good table and a flowing bowl. The sporting tourist sets out many bills of fare (notably one at p. 93), and Sir Walter affirms he would listen to Colonel Thornton over such a spread, but apparently not otherwise.

TODD, REV. JOHN (1763-1845): SPENSER, EDMUND (1553-1598),
WORKS OF. (1805) . . . . . Pr. xvii. 80

This was published in the *Edinburgh Review* for 1805. The reviewer enters his protest against a growing liking for variorum editions of great authors, in which the original author suffers by the mass of unsympathetic and contradictory views taken by those who stand as " five to one," and leave the poet crushed by the mere number of his commentators.

As Sir W. Scott says, the editors of variorum editions express their regard for the author as the Gauls showed their gratitude, " who overwhelmed with " their bucklers the virgin to whom they were indebted for the conquest of a " city."

TRISTREM, SIR : A METRICAL ROMANCE OF THE THIRTEENTH CEN-
TURY. (1804) . . . . Po. v.

Sir W. Scott never wavered in the belief that the " Sir Tristrem" of the Auchinleck manuscript was virtually if not actually the production of Thomas the Rhymer, Laird of Erceldoune, in Berwickshire, who flourished at the close of the thirteenth century. It was originally intended to include this in the " Minstrelsy," but it grew too bulky as Notes and Appendices were gath- ered together, and it was published as a separate work, of which Sir Walter retained the copyright. Second and third editions were published in 1806 and 1811. The copies in these editions numbered respectively one hundred and fifty, seven hundred and fifty, and one thousand. After that it was in- cluded in the collective editions of Scott's works.

The writer is sometimes called Lermont or Learmont, and sometimes " The " Rhymer." Erceldoune is a village in Berwickshire, a small distance from Melrose. There are many romances founded on the story of " Sir Tristrem," such as " Le Roman de Tristan" and " Iseult." The Auchinleck manuscript is a large and curious collection of romances made up of forty-four different pieces of poetry. " The date of the manuscript cannot possibly be earlier " and does not seem to be much later than 1330, at least eighty years after the " romance of ' Sir Tristrem' had been composed."

In appendix No. iv. (pp. 107–127) is given a short account of the forty- four pieces. The manuscript is a thick quarto, containing three hundred and thirty-four leaves. Some of the forty-four pieces are mere fragments, but others are works of great length. The romance of " Tristrem" was No. 37, and occupies nineteen leaves, but the " Conclusion" is wanting.

A *fac-simile* of the commencement of " Sir Tristrem" faces page 139.

The romance is in three fyttes, or acts, and Sir W. Scott has written a " Conclusion" (pp. 309–316) in imitation of the ancient " Rhymer," whoever he was, which " must always be admired as a remarkable specimen of skill " and dexterity."

" Thomas the Rhymer" survived in authorship mainly from his having been reputed to be a prophet and " a guide to the mysterious halls beneath " the Eildon Hills." He was called True Thomas from his prophecies enunciated after a three years' residence in perfect happiness with the Queen of Faery in Fairyland. His prophecies related to things that were to happen in the wars between England and Scotland. It is much disputed whether " Sir Tristrem" was written by him.

The poem is followed by a description and abstract (pp. 317–353) of two ancient fragments of French metrical romances on the subject of " Sir

"Tristrem" and an account (pp. 355–367), by Mr. Henry Weber, of the German romances founded on the story of "Sir Tristrem."

The volume closes with notes (pp. 369–462) and a glossary (pp. 463–493). On this writer, *see* also Po. iv. pp. 110–166.

TWO DROVERS, THE. (1827) . . . Nov. xli. 238–288

This is the second story of the first series of "Chronicles of the Canongate." The period of the story is 1765, in the time of George III. This tale Sir Walter learned from "an old friend, the late George Constable, of Wal- "lace-Craigie, near Dundee, whom he has already introduced to his readers "as the original Antiquary of Monkbarns." He had been "present at the "trial at Carlisle, and seldom mentioned the venerable judge's charge to the "jury without shedding tears." The old Scottish feeling of honour led to the taking a life for a blow, and when the punishment of the gallows had to be met the response made was, "I give a life for the life I took, and what "more can I do?"

TYTLER, PATRICK FRASER (1791–1849): SCOTLAND, HISTORY OF. Volumes i. and ii. (1829) . . . . Pr. xxi. 152

This review appeared in the *Quarterly* for November, 1829. This history was Mr. Tytler's principal work. It was published in nine volumes, 1828–43, and has a high reputation. Mr. Tytler was Professor of Universal History and Roman Antiquities at Edinburgh, and was afterwards created Lord Woodhouselee.

VISION OF DON RODERICK, THE. (1811) . . Po. ix. 355–440

This poem was written and published between April and July of 1811. It was a year in which subscriptions were taken up in aid of the Portuguese sufferers by the Bonaparte wars carried on upon the soil of that unfortunate country, and Scott wrote this poem as his subscription, and the "immediate pro- "ceeds were forwarded to the London Board."

It was afterwards inserted in the second volume of the *Edinburgh Annual Register*.

VOCAL POETRY; OR, A SELECT COLLECTION OF ENGLISH SONGS. BY JOHN AIKIN (1810) . . . . . Pr. xvii. 133

See Aikin.

[WALLADMOR: A ROMANCE. BY THE AUTHOR OF WAVERLEY. 3 vols. (1824.)

The romance entitled as above was a forgery (*see* Nov. xxxvii. p. xxix., *and* Lockhart's "Life," vol. vii. p. 385). It appeared at Leipsic in the German language, not as what it really was, a German novel, written by a German novelist, but as a translation from an English original by Sir W. Scott. Worse remained behind, for in that unhappy September, 1824, not only was the reading world not blessed with a " Waverley Novel," but instantly the forgery had been published in Germany the earliest copy was secured for the *London Magazine*, and De Quincey in " a few hours" reviewed it, quoting three passages out of its one thousand pages. By " pure accident," he tells us, " he " had stumbled upon almost every passage in the whole course of the thousand " pages which could be considered tolerable." The review pleased the publishers, and De Quincey was promptly commissioned to translate the whole book, and it was to be ready for the public " inside a month."

De Quincey's account of his translation into English of this German trash and of his alterations of the "almighty nonsense," of which " nine hundred " and fifty, to say the very least, of its thousand pages consisted," is as humourous, in the truest sense of the word, as anything he ever wrote. The three " corpulent German volumes collapsed into two English ones of rather con-" sumptive appearance."]

WALPOLE, HORACE (1716–1797), MEMOIR OF. (1821–25) Pr. iii. 299.

This is one of the " Prefaces" in Ballantyne's " Novelist's Library." Lord Orford, or, as he elected to be called, Horace Walpole, is probably best known by his letters. Macaulay says of him that " serious business was a trifle to " him, and trifles were his serious business." Sir W. Scott remarks that his most famous work, " Otranto," is remarkable as the first modern attempt to " found a tale of amusing fiction upon the basis of the ancient romances of " chivalry." It was ushered into the world in 1764 as " a translation by Wil-" liam Marshall from the Italian of Onuphrio Muralto, a sort of anagram or " translation of the author's own name." The secret of authorship was disclosed in the second edition. In a letter dated March 9, 1763, the author states that he " completed the tale in less than two months," doing away with the popular legend that it was written in eight days.

WATERLOO, THE FIELD OF. (1815) . . Po. xi. 255–291

See Field of Waterloo.

WAVERLEY. 2 vols. (1814) . . . . . Nov. i. *and* ii.

This was commenced in 1805, but laid aside after chapter vii. was written on an unfavourable opinion expressed by William Erskine. In 1810 the fragment was submitted to James Ballantyne, but he expressed very great doubts as to its probable success, and it was " forthwith laid aside again." In 1814 it was taken up once more, and the last two volumes of the original edition, which was in three volumes, were written in three weeks. Prescott has described it as " Shakespeare in prose." It was, as is well known, published anonymously, but " Jeffrey at once offered to make oath that it was Scott's."

Scott obstinately determined to keep the authorship a secret, and answered one of John Ballantyne's expostulations on the subject of "the secret" thus (*see* "Life," vol. iv. p. 179):

> " No, John, I will not own the book,—
> " I won't, you Piccaroon.
> " When next I try St. Grubby's brook,
> " The A. of Wa—— shall bait the hook,—
> " And flat-fish bite as soon
> " As if before them they had got
> " The worn-out wriggler,
>
> WALTER SCOTT."

The sale of forty thousand copies was attained by 1829, and, says Lockhart, well might Constable regret that he had not ventured to make up his offer of £700 to £1000 for the whole copyright of "Waverley," at which sum the author had been willing to trade. Fortunately for the latter, he netted several thousands instead of one by the over-caution of the publisher.

The author confesses that the tale "was put together with so little care that "he cannot boast of having sketched any distinct plan of the work." It relates to the insurrection in the Stuart interest led by Charles Edward in 1745.

The novel was dedicated by a "postscript which should have been a "preface" to the "Scottish Addison, Henry Mackenzie, by an unknown ad-"mirer of his genius." This was the celebrated Mackenzie (1745-1831), the author of "A Man of Feeling," that writer's most successful work.

The precautions taken to preserve the anonymity of Sir Walter are very curious. The original manuscript was transcribed under the publisher's eye by confidential persons, so that the author's handwriting never passed into the printing-room, and to that end double proof-sheets were regularly printed off, and the alterations made by the author were copied by Mr. Ballantyne, the publisher, by his own hand, upon the second proof-sheet, for the use of the printers, who in that way did not see the author's handwriting.

Scott's only reason for so long keeping up the secret was "by saying "with Shylock that such was my humour." The secret was well maintained, although known, says Sir W. Scott, "to not less than twenty "persons."

The particulars concerning the original secret and its avowal are contained in the "General Preface" to "Waverley" (Nov. i. pp. xx.–xl.) and the "In-"troduction to the 'Chronicles of the Canongate'" (Nov. xli. pp. iii.–lxxiii.).

"People" (writes James T. Fields) "who died prior to the 7th of July, "1814, were unfortunate in one respect if no other, for on that day was pub-"lished the first of the 'Waverley' romances. A world without Scott's "novels in it must have been rather a lean place to live in surely, and we can "never quite estimate the dulness and vacuity of a globe which existed before "that immortal story-teller was born into it." Sir Walter was forty-three years of age when he published "Waverley."

WILD HUNTSMAN, THE: TRANSLATION FROM BÜRGER . Po. vi. 307

This is "a translation, or, rather, an imitation of the 'Wilde Jäger' of "the German Poet Bürger." (*See* "Lenore.") It was originally published in 1796, and was then entitled "The Chace."

WITCHCRAFT, DEMONOLOGY AND, LETTERS ON. (1830.)

See Demonology.

WOMEN; OR, POUR ET CONTRE. BY MATURIN, REV. CHARLES ROB-
ERT. (1818) . . . . . . Pr. xviii. 172

See Maturin.

WOODHOUSELEE, LORD.

See Tytler.

WOODSTOCK; OR, THE CAVALIER. 2 vols. (1826) Nov. xxxix. *and* xl.

The romance is laid at the royal lodge of Woodstock and its vicinity in the time of the Commonwealth after the battle of Woodstock, "A Tale of "the Year Sixteen Hundred and Fifty One." Much interesting information as to Woodstock is to be found in Hone's "Every-Day Book," quoted largely from a tract entitled "The Genuine History of the Good Devil of "Woodstock, famous in the world, in the year 1649, and never accounted for "or at all understood to this time."

The novel is filled with historical personages,—*e.g.*, Joshua Bletson, one of the commissioners for the sequestration of Woodstock; the Duke of Buckingham, Charles II., Lord Clarendon, Oliver Cromwell, Colonel Desborough, General Harrison, and Sir Henry Lee, the ranger of Woodstock.

Sir W. Scott was writing this novel when his failure occurred. He determined to meet his losses bravely, and wrote a chapter a day whilst his bankruptcy was being arranged, and completed it on the sixty-ninth day after his ruin was announced.

In vol. xxxix. are given copies of two original pamphlets which contain a full account of the phenomena at Woodstock in 1649,—namely, the Woodstock Scuffle (pp. xxiii.-xxxv.) and the Just Devil of Woodstock (pp. xxxvi.-lxiv.). They were written in ridicule of the contractors or Parliament commissioners who went to sell the late king's lands, etc., at Woodstock.

YORK, FREDERICK, DUKE OF (1763–1827), MEMOIR OF. (1827) Pr.
iv. 400.

This was published in the *Edinburgh Weekly Journal* of January 10, 1827. The Duke of York was the second son of George III. He was commander-in-chief of the British forces for many years, and introduced many valuable reforms into the service. It relates with great care the consequences of the duke's liaison with Mrs. Clarke, his retirement from the high office of commander-in-chief in 1809, and his recall to that eminent position in 1811 which he occupied with distinction till the time of his death.

INDEX.

INDEX

www.ingramcontent.com/pod-product-compliance
Lightning Source LLC
Chambersburg PA
CBHW032150010726
47493CB00008BA/2649